GRAND VALLEY FEUD

Returning from the East to the family ranch, Jim Bannerman learns that his father has been killed by an unknown assailant. His brother Frank blames the murder on the sheepherders, and in particular on the Shaughnessy brothers. With the law proving ineffective, Jim sets out to bring the killer to justice and restore peace to the valley. But his attempts lead him into incredible danger as evil secrets are uncovered and a bloody feud erupts between the Bannermans and the sheepherders.

MARK BANNERMAN

GRAND VALLEY FEUD

Complete and Unabridged

LINFORD
Leicester

First   by

First Linford Edition
published 2000
by arrangement with
Robert Hale Limited
London

British Library CIP Data

Bannerman, Mark
  Grand Valley feud.—Large print ed.—
Linford western library
1. Western stories
2. Large type books
I. Title
823.9′14 [F]

ISBN 0-7089-5622-X

Published by
F. A. Thorpe (Publishing) Ltd.
Anstey, Leicestershire
Set by Words & Graphics Ltd.
Anstey, Leicestershire
Printed and bound in Great Britain by
T. J. International Ltd., Padstow, Cornwall

This book is printed on acid-free paper

1

The bell clanged as the store door was pushed open. Young Billy Clayton burst in, stumbling over the step. 'Bank's been raided!' he cried. 'Marshal Bouchel's rounding up a posse . . . swearing in everybody he can lay hands on.'

I was standing at the counter, my hands resting on a box of provisions. The storekeeper Jack Gibbon dropped his pencil and exclaimed, 'Bank raid, by golly! Never had no bank raid in Coltville afore.' He eyed me over the top of his spectacles. 'You better go lend a hand, Jim Bannerman.'

I nodded. Checking my Colt, I hurried from the store, unhitched my chestnut horse and got mounted. Billy Clayton had rushed on up the street, spreading the news. Down at the marshal's office I could see a crowd gathering. Everybody seemed to

1

be waving guns and shouting.

Coltville wasn't a big town. It had sprung up following a rumour that the railroad might head this way. But the railroad had never come, and Coltville was left to linger on. Apart from the bank, there was a saloon, a post-office, a town hall, a town-marshal's office, a church, and a few stores and houses. But despite its smallness, it was our town and we were proud of it — and if somebody had robbed the bank, feelings would sure run high.

As I joined the crowd outside the marshal's office, I realized that most of the pandemonium came from men shouting for others to keep quiet. Marshal Harry Bouchel, still spritely despite his sixty years, was standing on his verandah, a bible in his hand, and when eventually he could make himself heard he yelled: 'Everybody raise your right hand!' We all complied, and there and then he swore us in as United States Deputy Marshals. After that, everybody got mounted and we

2

rode down the street in a cloud of dust, white-faced women and old folks watching our departure, dogs yapping at the commotion. On the way, we passed Coltville's bank; a shaken-looking teller was standing on the step wringing his hands. 'Lynch them bastards!' he shouted.

There was maybe a dozen of us, including several sheepherders — Sam Crevis, Nat Shaughnessy, Mitch Edwards and some others I didn't know. I guess we didn't have much idea who we were chasing or where they'd gone. But Marshal Bouchel seemed to have a fair idea of the way our quarry had headed. Beneath me, I could feel my horse Copper's powerful stride. He'd been a gift from my pa for my nineteenth birthday, six months back.

Five miles out of town, we spotted a riderless horse waiting on the trail ahead, its reins hanging down, but as we approached it galloped off.

Reaching the spot where it had been, Bouchel raised his arm and we came to a halt. We all saw how the trail was splashed with blood — and it seemed to lead towards some nearby cottonwoods. Bouchel straightened in his saddle. 'Whoever was riding that animal was pretty badly wounded. Looks like he's crawled off into those trees.'

'Can't be one of them outlaws,' Mitch Edwards remarked. 'Weren't no gunfiring when the bank was robbed.'

Bouchel shook his head in puzzlement. 'Better have a look.'

We edged our horses apprehensively towards the trees, then drew rein. Bouchel nodded to me and three others. 'We'll go in and see if we can find anyone. The rest of you wait here.'

'Could be a trap, Marshal,' Nat Shaughnessy said.

'We'll soon find out,' Bouchel retorted drily, beckoning the three of us forward. Having dismounted we moved into the trees. It wasn't hard to follow the trail because there was wet-shiny blood on

4

the ground, and soon we heard groans coming from the bushes ahead.

We found the man sprawled against a tree, his hand clutching his chest, blood streaming through his fingers. He had a pained expression. I didn't reckon he had long left in this world, but that didn't seem to concern him; he was too busy cursing. 'Lousy bastard,' he muttered. 'Never figured he'd pull a gun on me.'

'Who pulled a gun?' Bouchel asked, leaning over him.

At last the wounded man seemed to comprehend that we represented the law. He groaned and rested back. 'If you want to catch the rest of them, they're making a rendezvous at Miller's Creek. That's where the loot's gonna be shared out, so Craig says.'

'Craig?' Bouchel said.

The outlaw nodded. 'Wint Craig. He figured I was finished. He deserves to be caught.'

'It was Craig who shot you, then?'

'Sure it was. Wint Craig — the

meanest bastard I ever knew. I wanted to split the cash here and scatter. Figured that was the best way to get away. But he went crazy — said he wouldn't have his orders questioned. I didn't agree . . . '

'And he gunned you down.' Bouchel filled in the story. 'How do I know you ain't feeding us a string of lies?'

The man sprawled before us gave a wry grin. 'You don't. When you get to Miller's Creek you'll find out, won't you?'

'If we walk into a trap,' Bouchel threatened, 'you'll be in serious trouble when we get back.'

'Not this side of the next world, Marshal. Now I'd be obliged if you'd let me die in peace.'

Despite his far-gone condition, a couple of men were detailed to take the wounded outlaw back to the doctor in town. The rest of us set out for Miller's Creek which was about twenty miles up the Ute River.

★ ★ ★

My pa, Edward Bannerman, owned the Double Horseshoe ranch in Grand Valley. Pa had told the story many times . . . how, with only a few steers, a wagon and six men, he'd staked his claim, fighting off Indians, sickness and the elements. He built his house with his own hands. Double Horseshoe grew from nothing to the best spread this side of the Smoke Mountains. That had been before my brother Frank, me and sister Mattie were born.

Our childhood had been pretty peaceful. Then the Shaughnessys showed up, grazing their sheep on the lush valley grass, and more sheepherders followed, pushing Pa back, claiming the good land across the river. My brother Frank always figured Pa had been soft-hearted and that he should have smashed them before they got too strong. Pa saw the danger too late.

But today I was riding alongside sheepherders, and our minds were set on bringing bank-robbers to justice.

We approached Miller's Creek in the late afternoon; sign on the trail indicated that the wounded outlaw had been telling the truth. He'd been so burned up with hatred for Wint Craig, clearly the gang leader, that he'd have lynched him himself if he'd been able.

At Miller's Creek, the river curved between high fern-covered banks. The surrounding ridges offered good vantage-points to see if anybody was coming up the main trail, and Marshal Bouchel suspected that Craig would have his lookouts posted. Accordingly he called a halt well back from the creek, and sent me and Nat Shaughnessy forward on foot to scout the creek. I grinned. I'd never dreamed that me and a sheepherder would ever be working together, trying to track down a common enemy.

Our big advantage was surprise. If Craig believed he had killed his ex-henchman, he wouldn't expect to be trailed to this place. So the two of us went cautiously through the trees, intending to reach the high ground overlooking the creek. Of course we knew we might be on a wild-goose chase. On the other hand, we might end up shooting it out with a gang of desperate men.

The sun was drifting westward when Shaughnessy and I reached the high ridge. We'd heard the clink of cooking-utensils and the murmur of voices, and we knew damned well that we'd struck lucky. Along the edge of the creek, we saw a small camp-fire, and squatting about it six men. Their horses were tethered in the trees.

Stealthily, we back-tracked to where Bouchel and the rest of the posse were rested up.

'Maybe we should wait till dark,' somebody suggested, 'then get them when they're bedded down.'

Bouchel shook his grey head. 'We ain't certain they'll stay here. After sharing out the loot, they'll most likely scatter. We'll strike now, boys. We'll get along both sides of the creek, then fire down on them.'

We nodded our agreement. I couldn't help wishing there was more of us, but as long as we had surprise on our side we were in with a chance.

The Marshal split us up, sending me and two other fellows down river, there to cross over and get along the far rim. Bouchel and the remaining force intended attacking from the near side of the creek.

Fifteen minutes later, I and my two companions had taken up position and were gazing down the slope towards the creek. We were thankful we hadn't waited for darkness. Already the outlaws were saddling their horses to move out. We immediately sprawled down on the rocks, took aim and opened fire. Almost simultaneously Bouchel's guns blasted out from the far side.

The outlaws were caught in our crossfire and three went down, but another two ran off into the cotton-woods.

Realizing that our job from this side of the creek was done, we scrambled down through the ferns, hollering to Bouchel that we were coming. We waded across the creek. An oulaw who'd survived the crosswhip of bullets had his hands raised. Bouchel and another member of the posse charged off into the trees, in pursuit of the men who'd run off — and we soon heard pistol-fire.

Excitement was pumping inside me, and it seemed that everything had been too easy. The sound of shooting had me blundering in Bouchel's wake into the trees. Suddenly I found myself on the edge of a clearing — with a man's back turned towards me. I pulled up, holding my breath. From the far side of the clearing, Bouchel's voice boomed out: 'This is Marshal Bouchel. We got you covered Craig. Get your hands raised!'

The man with his back to me

11

stiffened. 'Okay, Marshal,' he called in a deep voice. 'You've caught us fair and square.' He lifted his hands slightly. Right then I noticed there was a pistol tucked in his belt.

As Bouchel stepped from the trees, his pistol levelled, Craig jerked into motion, throwing himself to the side, his hand clawing for the pistol. The marshal, not being so fast as he was, was caught by the speed of the outlaw. Bouchel fired but missed, would've fired again but his hammer clicked on an empty chamber. Meanwhile Craig clambered up, raising his pistol, knowing that he had the marshal at his mercy. Harry Bouchel braced himself for the shot.

I fired. The bullet took Craig in the shoulder, throwing him forward, sending his pistol flying. Bouchel immediately dived on top of him, and I joined him as we snapped handcuffs over the wrists of the writhing outlaw.

'My God, Jim,' Bouchel gasped. 'You saved my skin. I'm sure grateful.'

I would have enjoyed my moment of glory, had Craig not turned, blood pumping from his shoulder, and fixed me with his stare. I'd never seen such fury, such downright evil burning in a man's eyes. 'One day,' he hissed, 'I'll make every man in this posse pay for what's happened. I'll rip your whole damned valley apart! *And you, kid, especially you, will wish you'd never been born! That's a promise*!'

The menace of his threat had my stomach churning.

★ ★ ★

My father had a strong, weather-beaten face and hair that had gone iron-grey since my mother's death three years earlier. He'd reared Frank and me with a firm hand, though he'd always been fair. He had a particularly soft spot for Mattie. I knew he was proud of what I'd done on the day of the robbery, though he never told me to my face. They made me out to be quite a hero

13

in the local newspaper, especially at the time of the trial, when Winston Craig got a ten-year sentence in the state pen.

A month after the bank robbery, Pa beckoned me into his office. He sat behind his desk, which was spread with bills and papers relating to Double Horseshoe business.

'Jim,' he said waving me into a chair, 'I've had a letter from Ed Cutillo. You probably remember me talking about him. He was a real good friend to the Bannermans in the early days. He helped finance us when I was buying stock. Couldn't have done it without him.'

I nodded, wondering what he was getting at.

'Well, Ed's got his own freighting business in the East now. He's in the process of moving it from New York to Boston. The problem is, he's in need of able-bodied assistance for maybe two, three years. I was wondering if you'd like to see the East. I know you'd work hard.'

The suggestion surprised me. I'd always figured my future lay here on the ranch, working alongside Pa and Frank.

'Of course it'd make no difference to the inheritance,' he went on. 'Everything'd be split three ways between Frank, you and Mattie. It'd sure ease my conscience if you went, Jim. It'd be like settling an old debt, and anyway, I guess Ed'll pay well.'

The prospect of seeing the East had always appealed to me — but the thought of having to leave Janet Shaughnessy behind gnawed at me. I wondered if one of the reasons Pa wanted me to go east was to stop my relationship with her developing. 'Damned sheep have no right in Grand Valley!' were his often repeated words.

In the early days, when there'd been only the Shaughnessys and two other sheepherding families in the valley, things had gone well enough. Pa, feeling sorry for them, had allowed them to scrape a living off his land.

15

But by the time we kids got around to attending the schoolhouse in Coltville, feelings had begun to run high. More sheepherders had moved in, building their cabins and flooding the land with their sheep.

At school we'd all got along together same as any other kids; we were too young to understand our folks' dislike of one another. Janet and I hit it off from the day I brought my pony to school and allowed her to ride him. After that we were together most of the time.

I felt sure that a few years' separation wouldn't change the way Janet and I felt about each other. And the prospect of building up some savings would mean that we'd be able to start married life on a better footing, but I didn't tell my father what was in my mind.

'Sure,' I said. 'If it'll help you, I'll go east.'

★ ★ ★

A few days before I left, Coltville held its homely Independence Day celebrations. It was great to see the Bannermans and the sheepherders rubbing shoulders as if there'd never been any trouble, just as we had on the day of the robbery. Come evening, there was a concert in the town hall. That was a real night to remember. My brother Frank cast off his usual seriousness and his dry humour had everybody laughing, especially when the liquor flowed. Yes, my brother looked mighty handsome that night, catching the eyes of all the pretty girls — apart from Janet's. Her eyes were for me alone, and I was so excited by her nearness that I paid little attention to either the concert or the liquor.

With the fiddles playing merrily, I took Janet in my arms, and the touch of her seemed strangely different, now that she wore a dress — flared and yellow — instead of her customary work-shirt and Levis.

Before long, we'd edged to the door, longing for the coolness beneath the stars. In the shadow of the porch her hand tightened on mine. Her lips rose willingly to mine . . . Then came the sound of footsteps in the doorway behind us, and Janet pulled from my embrace. I cursed the person who had crossed the verandah, and Janet laughed softly, her teeth showing white in the lamp-wash.

'It's too doggone crowded here,' I whispered.

'Yes, honey,' she laughed.

From down by the horse-trough, my horse Copper nickered his recognition as we approached.

'If you was dressed in your proper clothes,' I murmured, 'we could go riding.'

'Don't you like me this way, Jim?'

'You're too boyish for frills,' I teased, while inwardly I was thinking just the opposite. She'd been the prettiest girl in the hall.

'Then you'll have to take me home,

so I can get changed!' With that she pulled me towards the chestnut, and I mounted up and lifted her across the saddle in front of me. As we edged forward, her head turned a little so that my lips could brush her cheek.

'It's real cosy on the one horse, Jim,' she said.

Neither of us had the least intention of going to her home. We headed in the opposite direction. Soon the boisterous scraping of the dance-hall violins had given way to the whisper of the night-breeze in the tree-tops. The only other sound came from the steady plod of the chestnut's hooves. The moon painted the land silver.

'Everything's so peaceful,' Janet murmured. 'I wish it could always be this way.'

'I reckon the only way to make Grand Valley peaceful,' I said, 'is for the Bannermans and the sheepherders to get together more often. What we need hereabouts is twenty or so Independence Days a year.'

'A wedding might help some,' she murmured.

'I love you, Janet, and there'll be a wedding for sure. Just be patient a while longer and trust me.'

'But have you *got* to go to New York?'

Here it was again — the sore point. 'Trust me, Janet.' I repeated. 'Try to understand that I owe this to Pa. I want to do what's right.'

For a minute she was silent, but when she next spoke, her words had me loving her more than ever. 'If you think it's right, Jim, then I think it's right too. It was selfish of me to try and make you change your mind, but it was only because I love you so much. Just remember, I'll be waiting, just as long as you want me.'

Soon we were laughing again. We both knew that we wouldn't have many more hours together before my departure, and we were determined that no sadness should spoil these precious moments.

With Janet so close, her head snuggled against my shoulder, I'd not noticed where the chestnut's ambling was taking us; now he trailed to a halt and dipped his muzzle into water; we were at the river. The spot was an old haunt of ours, where big boulders jutted out into the water and the bank was clustered with willows.

The night was warm and the water looked cool and inviting. As we dismounted, Janet swung to face me. 'Jim, let's have a swim!'

'We ain't dressed for swimming,' I grinned.

'Turn around and face that tree, Jim Bannerman,' she ordered impishly. 'Just stay that way till I say it's okay. Don't you dare turn round before I say so!'

'Now would I do such a thing?' I protested, turning to face the willows; she didn't answer.

I heard the rustle of her dress, and then seconds later the swish of water as she waded in. Right then I figured she wouldn't be looking my way, so, telling myself what a cheat I was, I stole a glance over my shoulder. I wasn't disappointed.

She was no more than knee-deep in water, with the moonlight on her slender figure. Her body was faultless, with wide, straight shoulders and a waist as slim as a child's. Her hips were narrow and her thighs rounded. For a moment I stood spellbound, obsessed by my good fortune in having such a lovely girl for my own.

As she dipped down, submerging herself in the water and gasping at the coolness, I swung back. 'You can come now, Jim!' Her demure innocence increased my shame.

I pulled off my clothes and followed her in, and when the freshness of the water had reached my thighs she twisted round. Her head was thrown back provocatively, and when she spoke her voice had lost its innocence. 'You big cheat, Jim Bannerman!'

With that, she pushed hard against

my chest, the unexpected shove sending me over backwards with a terrific splash. I swallowed a gallon of river-water and surfaced to the sound of her laughter. Gasping for breath, I vowed vengeance. Still laughing, she swam swiftly away with me fast in pursuit.

For a half-hour we splashed and chased about in that mountain-fresh water, making enough noise for a whole Indian tribe taking its annual dip. Janet quit the water first, drying herself with the blanket which had been tied to my saddle. When I followed her out, she'd put on her dress and was fixing her hair.

After I'd dressed she slipped her hands around my neck. 'I don't think I've ever been happier, Jim.'

'Nor me,' I murmured. 'I wish we could stay here forever and forget about the rest of the world.'

I pulled her hips into mine, and she came willingly, pressing the firm swell of her breasts against my chest. Her parted lips came hungrily to mine. Her dress slipped back from her shoulders, and I realized she had deliberately left it unfastened. Beneath it she was naked. 'O-oh, honey . . . ' she moaned as we lowered our bodies to the welcoming softness of the bank.

In the warmth of that July night, in the willows flanking the river, so strong was our love that it seemed nothing would ever break it.

* * *

Two days later I bade farewell to Pa and Mattie. Pa gave me a hug, which was something he'd never done before, and it made a lump come into my throat. Frank was taking me in a wagon to Coltville where I was to catch the stage. As I gazed over my shoulder for a last look at the ranch, I little dreamed that my world would never be the same again, that so much relating to my childhood and early manhood was to be shattered.

2

It was three years later. Pa's long-standing debt to Ed Cutillo had been paid off with my sweat. Now, a couple of hours' ride would see me back at the Double Horseshoe.

Mattie had never been much for letter-writing, and that was why when her letter had caught up with me in Boston, I'd guessed something was wrong. Sure enough the very worst had happened. Pa was dead.

On top of this, outright warfare between cattlemen and sheepherders had erupted.

Heavy of heart, I was gripped by the angry grief which had come upon me so often during the journey back. Why had this happened? Why was my father dead? I climbed into the saddle of the sorrel I'd purchased in Dalton, forded the Ute River and rode into the hills beyond. Soon sheep were scattering nervously before me, as if they knew I was a Bannerman. When I was clear of the flock I headed down an arroyo which formed a natural-made trail into the valley. The day's heat was slackening and familiar sounds greeted me: the silvery notes of a meadow-lark and the friendly chatter of pinon squirrels.

Halfway down the arroyo was a large pocket, into which had been built the Mulheron cabin. In years gone by the Mulherons had been the paupers of the sheepherding fraternity. Things had changed; the original abode, a rough, mud-and-grass soddy, had given way to a fine cedar-log cabin.

A thick-set youngster gazed at me and then ran back inside. I kneed the sorrel forward, not wishing to meet Paddy Mulheron or his wife Sarah. Any greeting they extended would hardly take the form of a welcome home.

Instead of emerging at the foot of the arroyo, I mounted the bank into the cottonwoods. I felt weary and I wanted to avoid any sheepherders, so I kept to the cover of the timber. Eventually I had to quit the trees to cross the cut-back of the river. The whinny of a horse had me wrenching my sorrel back into the trees.

I heard the bleating of sheep, and soon Sam Crevis and his brother Tom rode into view, driving a flock of about fifty ahead of them. Sam's eyes were alert and a Winchester rifle was slanted across his saddle. He was a big, hard-muscled man, his shirt sagging open to reveal the dark hair of his chest. His face was mean and his hands gripped the gun as though he hankered to use it.

Tom, the younger of the two, was a smaller man, made ugly by a bad cast in his eye. He toted a hand-gun and had a rifle in his saddle-scabbard.

Three years ago I would have exchanged a nod, but now I was glad enough to remain hidden and let them pass. Mattie's letter had left no doubt in my mind that bitter hatred had flared up. I waited five minutes, then nudged the sorrel forward. The sheep-noise had faded into the distance and ahead of me the sweeping arm of the river glistened. But between the trees and the water on the uneven floor of the valley, something caught my eye. The sorrel tried to rear back but I forced him on.

Scattered beside the river were what seemed like some thirty dirty-grey boulders. The air had lost its freshness and fat blow-flies were clouding up.

Drawing closer, I realized the 'boulders' were sun-bloated, buzzard-picked sheep carcasses, and these stretched for about fifty yards along the river bank. Buzzards had ripped at the flesh, but the flies still found plenty to fuss over. The stench was vile enough to indicate the butchery wasn't many days old. The ground was strewn with spent cartridge-cases. I could picture the beasts panicking as bullets felled them.

I had no desire to linger. I edged

through the carcasses and crossed the river.

On the far bank, the broad swell of the valley stretched into the far distance — a vast green vale, broken only occasionally by knolls, each clothed with its stand of pines — Bannerman country!

I was anxious to get my homecoming done with. From Frank I would learn what was going on in Grand Valley. Pa dead, sheep butchered, sheep-herders ugly-faced and heavily armed — what did it all add up to? And where did the Shaughnessys figure — particularly Janet?

Janet . . . The old sickening feeling increased my misery. It came upon me every time I thought of her, which was plenty. I kept telling myself that it was all over, that she didn't want me any longer. With not a single answer to my letters, it seemed obvious she'd fallen for somebody else. And yet somehow I couldn't bring myself to believe it. My longing for her had increased as time went on, undimmed by the fancy women of New York and Boston. Right now I wanted her more than ever.

Away in the distance I saw cattle grazing, and amongst them occasional horsemen. I wondered what changes had three years brought to the Double Horseshoe? What changes would Pa's death have brought?

For ten minutes I cut west, then as the ground began lifting steeply beneath the sorrel's hooves I dismounted and led him on up a brush-clothed knoll. On top was a cluster of pines.

It was just over the crest, just down beyond the trees in a flat, sheltered spot, that I found what I sought. Years ago Ma had been buried here, and now close to her grave there was fresh-turned soil. A second cross had been erected. Its inscription hammered the bitterness of renewed grief into my soul . . .

HERE LIES EDWARD BANNERMAN
MURDERED JUNE 20 1887
BY A HAND UNKNOWN

3

I don't know how long I sat by the grave. I could imagine Pa's deep voice booming out of the past, telling men to ride herd, to get the wagon rolling, to break camp. I could see Pa, big and tall, riding across the range — his range. I could recall folks looking at me as I passed and telling each other, 'That's Ed Bannerman's boy.' I had held my head higher then, a tingle of pride in me.

I stepped away from the grave and gazed at the Double Horseshoe buildings spread beneath me, two-hundred yards down the slope. Apart from a few additional outhouses, it hadn't changed much since I'd last seen it. The bunk-houses were along the eastern side of the fine cedar-wood house with its white-painted verandah. At the back of the house were the peeled-log ramblings of hayricks, the feed and foaling sheds and the stables. Pa had loved fine-bred beasts, both horses and cattle.

The whole place had been built in the lee of the knoll on which I now stood, and thus escaped the fury of the cold winter winds. Now, smoke was curling up from the chimneys of the main house. The smell of cooking carried up on the still air and had me licking my lips.

I became aware of hooves pounding down in the valley. Six riders were heading for the ranch. As they drew closer I recognized Frank, tall in his saddle, and close behind him rode the Mexican Carlos Vasquez, a long-serving retainer of the Bannerman family.

I felt glad to see Frank. Sometimes, when in a serious mood, he reminded me of Pa. As a youngster he'd often scared me with his changes of mood, but Pa seemed to understand Frank, and as we grew older I reckoned I did as well.

I unsheathed my Remington, then I turned it skywards and pulled the trigger. The crack of the shot brought the riders to a halt below me, and I took off my Stetson and waved it in the air.

Frank returned my wave. Gesturing for his men to go on into the ranch, he turned his mount towards the knoll and minutes later reined to a stop and dismounted.

We stood looking at each other, both strangely at a loss for words. I noticed how he'd aged. Lines of worry showed about his eyes. The scar on his forehead, a result of a brawl years ago with Sam Crevis over a girl, showed up angry-looking on his forehead. Even so, the old handsomeness was still there.

He reached out and grabbed my hand, somehow raising a smile of welcome. 'Jim, I didn't want to drag you back into all this trouble. I wanted to let things settle before you got the news, but Mattie insisted on writing.'

'How did it happen?' I asked. 'How did Pa die?'

His smile faded. He turned away, paced towards the grave and stood looking down at it. 'Carlos found him, Jim, at Peakman's Gulley.' He turned to face me, his eyes blazing with anger. 'He'd been shot in the back.'

'But why? Who . . . ?'

'I was in Coltville with Hilda when Ben Wells brought the news. I couldn't believe him. It didn't seem possible. They'd got Pa's body back at the house when I got home. There were three slugs in him, two between the shoulder-blades and one near his kidneys. Marshal Dainton came over soon as he heard.'

'Marshal Dainton?' I interrupted.

'Yeah. Dainton took over as town marshal when Harry Bouchel retired. We went over Peakman's Gulley with a fine-tooth comb, but there was nothing. The marshal searched the sheepherders' cabins, but he couldn't prove anything. All the same, it's clear the damned

34

sheepherders did it.' Frank's voice was hoarse, as though it hurt his throat. 'They'd no right here in the first place. I swear I'll drive every one of them off this land. Pa won Grand Valley. He was here before anybody else.'

After a moment I asked, 'Who gunned Pa down, then?'

There was quiet conviction in his reply. 'The Shaughnessys have been at the back of all the trouble in this valley, them and the Crevis brothers. Wipe them out, and we'll have wiped out Pa's killer.'

I gripped the horn of my saddle, letting his words soak in, then I mounted the sorrel. 'How come all those sheep were butchered across the river, Frank?'

He climbed into his saddle. 'Boys took the notion to have themselves a little revenge. Hell, I wish they'd burned a few cabins at the same time!' He glanced at me. 'Let's get down to the house. You must be dog-tired.'

Minutes later, faces were peering at

35

us as we rode through the outhouses, but none were familiar. I saw my sister Mattie, slim and pretty in jeans and red hickory shirt. She came running towards us. She was much changed from the gangling youngster I could remember. She was a woman now, full-fledged, all of nineteen years.

Behind her welcoming smile was the same anxiety I'd seen in Frank, but she must have realized I'd had more than enough grief on my home-coming because, as we dismounted, she hurled herself into my arms. I whirled her round, then set her down to get a good look at her.

'Wow,' I laughed, 'you've sure changed some. Still got the same turned-up nose, though!'

I watched the old indignation rise in her eyes, but she laughed and said, 'Here were we expecting a fine eastern dude, and look what arrives — Chief Ouray hisself!'

Maybe I did look like a Ute Indian. I'd always been blessed with a dusky complexion, high cheek-bones and a hatchet nose, though heaven knows how I'd come by my looks because there was no Indian blood in my ancestry.

'Meester Jim!' A croaking and familiar voice had me turning. Carlos Vasquez thrust his leathery hand into mine, its partner thumping my back. 'Eet is good you come home. You are needed here very much now.'

I glanced towards the Vasquez cabin which adjoined one of the barns. Several dark-skinned children were playing in the doorway.

'I heard there was a fourth Vasquez,' I said.

Carlos looked hurt. 'Feeth, please Meester Jim — and soon there will be another!'

'Good old Maria,' I laughed. Maria was the Mexican's Ute wife. 'Where is she?'

Mattie took my arm. 'She's getting chow ready. Come on in. You must be hungry as a bull-calf.'

Carlos took the horses away, and Frank led us in through the open doors of the house. Home, I thought, how can it be home without Pa?

Mattie was soon leading me up to my room. I gave her the books I'd brought her from the east. Briefly, her eyes shone with gratitude. But then she suddenly changed, and I realized how great a strain this forced cheerfulness had been to her.

'I don't know what we'd have done if you hadn't come, Jim,' she sobbed. 'Frank was angry when I told him I'd written to you, but I thought it was right you should know. Now that there are only three of us Bannermans left, we must stick together. Since the law can't help us, we've got to punish Pa's killer ourselves.'

'Mattie, I'd never have forgiven you if you hadn't written.' I gently pushed her back onto a chair and stepped across to the window. The sun was slipping into the west. From the bunk-houses came the burble of men's voices. The uneven line of the hills was visible above the pine-topped knoll where Pa was buried, hazed into blue by the distance. Somewhere up there were the cabins of the sheepherders, among them the Shaughnessys' place.

'They're very strong now,' Mattie said, reading my thoughts. 'There are eight families — more than ever.'

I asked: 'Have you heard anything about Janet?'

Mattie caught her breath. There was a pleading in her eyes as they met mine. After a moment she said quietly, 'Forget about her, Jim. She's a Shaughnessy, and Frank says it's them who murdered Pa. We must . . . '

'Janet,' I said, 'have you heard word of her?'

Mattie bit her lip, then she nodded. 'It's the talk of the valley . . . about her and Sam Crevis.'

'Sam Crevis!' The name burst from my lips. Crevis, the hard-muscled sheepherder I'd seen that very afternoon riding shotgun over his herd. He was handsome right enough — but him and Janet! The thought sickened me.

Mattie took hold of me again. 'Forget about her, Jim. None of them are any good. Frank's right; we've got to drive them out so they can't do us no more harm.'

I was fighting to control my anger. Forget Janet. God, how could I! After a while I asked, 'What's the law been doing? This Marshal Dainton — is he plumb useless?'

Mattie scoffed. 'There's no law in this valley, not since Marshal Bouchel went and that no-good Jim Dainton took over. He'll never bring anybody to justice — and I'm beginning to think Gregg is just as useless.'

Gregg Miller was Mattie's stepping-out friend, had been as long as I could remember. He also happened to be Coltville's deputy marshal.

'I've told Gregg I don't want to see him again,' Mattie went on, 'not until the law finds Pa's killer.' Her voice had a bitter edge on it. She moved towards the door, but before she left she turned and her voice was soft again. 'I'm sorry to be such a misery now you've come home. I'd planned things so differently.'

When I'd rid myself of my stubble, washed and changed my clothes, the old Spanish gong sounded from downstairs, announcing that it was time to feed. Maria and Mattie had worked wonders, determined to make a small celebration out of my home-coming. Home-reared yearling loin-beef had seldom tasted so good.

There were eight of us at the table that night, but apart from Frank and Mattie I knew only Ben Wells of old. He was the ranch-foreman — a big, raw-boned Texan with a tangled mass of straw-coloured hair.

Frank introduced me to the other four: Ed Hunter, a man with striking green eyes; Jess Fulcher, who had long flowing white hair; Hank Symes, an ex-cavalry sergeant; and finally Tom

Glint, a Chiricahua Apache. They were all top-hands, taken on during the time I'd been away.

Often during that meal my mind started to drift, and looking up towards the head of the table it seemed odd to see Frank and not Pa sitting there. Frank and I were partners now in the Double Horseshoe, but the circumstances in which this had come about dampened any pride I might have felt. Frank had assumed control and it shouldn't have worried me seeing him stepping into Pa's shoes — he had more right than me, sure enough — but all the same, an uncomfortable feeling settled in on me.

When the plates had been emptied, Frank produced a bottle of Spanish wine. For a while we drank in silence, then he leaned across the table towards me. 'I reckon we're gonna have our chance to get at the sheepherders mighty soon. 'Specially now you're here, Jim.'

Ben Wells glanced at me. 'You'd better strap on a gun, Jim. Ain't no telling when you'll need it.'

I nodded. 'Seems no good relying on the law.'

Later, when Mattie was busy washing up, Frank and I stepped outside for a breather. From the velvety darkness came sounds of life: from the bunk-houses the raucous laughter of men; from the Vasquez cabin the cry of a baby. From further away sounded the eerie call of a ground-owl. Also out there on the range were the silent masses of Double Horseshoe cattle, and about them, I knew, would be heavily-armed guards, riding at Frank's command, ready for any move the sheepherders might make.

Frank fixed himself a cigarette, then passed the tobacco-pouch to me. As we lit up, leaning back against the corral fence, he said, 'Guess you figure I been high-handed here since Pa was killed.' He took a draw on his cigarette, then went on. 'There's one thing more you'd better know, Jim. I guess you'll find it hard to agree with, though. These damned sheepherders are strong, and sure as hell there's gonna be a big fight soon. I don't intend to lose. I got to figuring we should have somebody around who could really use a gun.'

He paused. We could both hear the sound of horses approaching. A minute later three men rode into the Double Horseshoe, three hulking shadows in the blackness. I caught the snatch of a low, throaty laugh. The newcomers dismounted, stabled their animals and then went into a bunk-house. I figured they were three of our normal hands, just in off duty.

'Go on, Frank,' I prompted. 'Surely you haven't hired Wyatt Earp?'

He shuffled his feet. 'No, Jim, but the man I've hired is just as fast. That was him — the big hombre who laughed. He's been in Coltville this evening. He's the man we need to scare the sheepherders. Jim . . . Wint Craig is helping us out.'

I gasped. I suddenly felt as though somebody had rammed a fist into my belly.

4

That night I dreamed of Janet, laughing and happy in Sam Crevis's arms. Then Frank came upon them, his eyes all fiery. 'Sam,' he rasped, 'you gave me this scar on my head, now I'm gonna kill you!' All at once his gun was belching flame. Suddenly Wint Craig was there, and his gun was drawn too — but he was turning it on me. I awoke with a shout.

Soon, far removed from sleep, I got up, sat in a chair and made myself a smoke. There were a few things I had to get clear in my mind.

Frank seemed sure the Shaughnessys were behind Pa's death; and Jenny's talk about Sam Crevis and Janet had rocked me to the very roots. By daybreak my mind was made up. Frank maybe had his faults, but what he was planning was for the good of

46

the Bannermans. It was up to me to help him all I could. Still, before he attacked the sheepherders, I was going to ride up to the Shaughnessy cabin and ask old John Shaughnessy outright if he knew anything about Pa's death — and hear from Janet's lips whether or not she was finished with me.

I dressed, then went to the cupboard in the corner of the room. Inside, I found a package swathed in oilskins. I untied the leather thongs, ripped aside the greasy wrappings and took out my gunbelt. Three years it had lain idle; now was the time to put it to use again.

I buckled on the belt, then I picked up the Colt .44. Once, hours of tin-can practice had had me pretty slick with a gun, but now I'd probably got a bit rusty. Even so, the cold hardness of the walnut butt fitted snugly in my palm, and slipping the Colt into its holster, I knew I could gun a man down if I had to.

After breakfast I told Frank I'd like

to see the place where Pa had been murdered.

'We've already searched Peakman's Gulley,' he frowned. 'Ain't no point in poking around there again.'

'I want to see for myself,' I insisted.

Anger showed in his eyes, but he shrugged his shoulders. 'Okay,' he conceded. 'Won't do no good, though. I guess I'll ride with you.'

'Thanks, Frank, but firstly I'm gonna see if Carlos has been taking good care of that Copper horse of mine.'

I was relieved to see Frank smile. 'Cared for him like one of his own papooses! When you're ready we'll get moving.' He turned and walked towards the house.

A group of men came out of the bunk-house; among them was the tall, black-garbed figure of Wint Craig. He had two ivory-butted Colts strapped low on his thighs. He'd been laughing, but the laugh died on his lips as he spotted me. I thought he was going to walk over to me, but he seemed to change his mind. He turned back to his companions and they untethered and mounted their horses and spurred out onto the range.

Suddenly aware of the cries of children, I noticed three of Carlos Vasquez's offspring playing in the dust in front of his cabin. They quietened as I approached, and their Ute-sharp eyes swung towards me. The oldest of them, nine-year-old Pedro, suddenly grinned and the others lost their apprehension. They took hold of my hands and hustled me through the door of the cabin. Inside was Maria, Carlos's woman.

She was a full-blooded Ute Indian, and the passing years had not robbed her of her wild beauty. Even at this moment, heavy with child, she looked radiantly happy to see me. Barely were our greetings over before she had filled a cup of wine for me.

'Drink to the end of sadness,' she said.

'The wound will always be there,

Maria,' I murmured.

'But time dulls the pain, Meester Jim.'

I drank, feeling the warmth of the wine surge through me. Carlos came in from the other room. He took the wine Maria offered him and drank with me.

'I've come for my horse, Carlos,' I told him.

'Ah, Copper. He has been impatient for your return, Meester Jim.' He reached for his sombrero, rammed it on his head, and with a glint in his eye said, 'Come.'

There was no doubt that Copper remembered me. He let out a whinny that shook the stable rafters. Soon I had my double-cinched Texas saddle on his back and I mounted up.

'You've looked after him well, Carlos,' I said, eyeing the healthy gloss of Copper's chestnut coat.

'How else could I treat such a horse, Meester Jim!'

Carlos mounted his own roan and

edged in alongside me. 'I theenk I know where we go now,' he said, and the cheerfulness had drained from his voice.

We crossed the yard to where Frank was mounted and waiting for us. It didn't please me to see that Mattie was with him. There was no need to add to her grief, and as we came up to them I told her so.

Turning her brown eyes full on me, she replied in a stubborn voice: 'I'm going with you because I want to, Jim,' and it was pointless to argue.

We left the ranch at the gallop, Frank leading the way, then Mattie riding beside me, and Carlos following.

We skirted the big, pine-topped knoll and swung out onto the broad flat of the valley. The sun was hot, the sky cloudless blue, and the hills across the river looked deceptively close. At last, the Ute River, a sun-glistening ribbon, showed ahead of us.

There were no sounds other than the thump of hooves and the rhythmic

51

creak of the stirrup-leathers. We didn't talk; our minds were too full of where we were going and what had happened there. Peakman's Gulley ... I remembered the place well enough. Now its memory was like a dark shadow across my soul. I realized that this was the same trail as Pa had followed on that fateful day.

There was no mystery as to why he'd gone to Peakman's Gulley; everybody knew that this was the place he chose when he wanted to be alone, maybe to dream about the old days when he'd brought his young wife to the valley to carve a future out of the wilderness. He took off once, maybe twice, a week when work wasn't too heavy, to have a peaceful hour with his pipe and his memories. All his killer had had to do was wait . . .

We passed scattered groups of Texas longhorn cattle, giant beasts as wild as bob-cats. I wondered where my brother was grazing the Double Horseshoe's prize Herefords and I asked him.

'I've got 'em up at the Coyote Lake range,' he replied. 'It's the best summer grazing, and they're out of the way of any devilment the sheepherders might plan. Seems like we're gonna make a fine fortune out of them Herefords come the fall, Jim.'

As we followed the river, the banks gradually steepened into the hills that were thick with cottonwoods. Close to Peakman's Gulley, we left the river and cut through the timber. We halted in a clearing, and Frank twisted to face us. His eyes had a strange wildness. 'Let's go on in afoot,' he said huskily.

We dismounted. I turned to Mattie. 'Stay here with the horses. There's no need for you to come right into the gulley. It'd only upset you.'

This time she didn't argue but reached out and took the reins. There were tears in her eyes.

Carlos came up and laid a gentle, understanding hand on her shoulder before following Frank and me through the trees and out onto the rock-strewn slope which led to Peakman's Gulley. It was a steep climb, and for the last few yards the gradient was devoid of rocks.

Once at the top, we could see down into the gulley. Natural ledges projected almost step-like from its sides, which were covered with outjuts of greasewood bushes. A zigzag path led into the gulley's depths, where the river flowed. Narrow strips of yellow sand lined the river's banks, petering off into the shrubbery and rock.

'Eet was down there, close to the water, that I found Señor Bannerman,' Carlos explained. 'He had fallen from up here somewhere.'

A stillness hung over the gulley; even the river flowed silently. Glancing at the rims, I saw that there were boulders and brush enough to conceal a whole army.

Frank led the way down. When we were standing in the soft sand, he said, 'Pa was sprawled just here, with his head towards the water. That right, Carlos?'

'*Si, señor.*'

Frank pointed towards the opposite gulley-side. 'Shots must have been fired from up there.'

'Did you get the shells out of his body?' I asked.

Frank nodded. 'Sure. But they didn't give us a clue, Jim. Just ordinary shells same as any of us use.'

I turned to Carlos. 'What time did you find him?'

'Six in the evening. He'd gone out in the morning, said he'd be back by noon. In the afternoon I started to worry. Meester Frank was in town. I didn't know when he'd be back, so I decided to look for heem.'

I nodded towards the far rim. 'Think maybe I'll take a look at where you figure the shots came from.'

'Go ahead,' Frank grunted, 'but you're wasting your time, Jim. Carlos and me'll wait here.'

Unreasonable as it was, I felt I had

to go over every inch of the ground in the hope that I might find some clue the others had missed. I pulled off my shirt and boots, unbuckled my gunbelt and slipped out of my Levis, then, naked, waded into the water and swam across to the opposite bank. I scrambled through the bushes.

What was it I hoped to fine? Footmarks? A cigarette butt? Even as I searched I realized what a fool I was being. Many people had been to this place since the killing; the wind and rain had removed any traces that might have been missed. Frank was right: I'd find nothing that would help us.

I reached the top, and twisted round to see Frank and Carlos, their hands shading their eyes, looking up at me from across the river.

'That would've been the place, Meester Jim!' Carlos's voice echoed slightly in the gulley.

The ground shelved back where I was standing into an almost trench-like groove; an ideal hideaway for the murderer. There was even a smooth rock on which to steady his rifle. I had a mental picture of my father, his back turned, clambering down the path . . . and then the sudden, hateful crack of the killer's gun!

Suddenly I felt sick. The answer to Pa's death wouldn't be found here. Frank was right — had been all along. We would find the guilty party up in the sheepherders' cabins. But then I got thinking about Wint Craig, and after that I wasn't so sure about anything.

Frank and Carlos were hunkered down smoking as I came out of the water again. I pulled on my clothes. Frank stood up and tossed aside his smoke.

'Guess Mattie'll be wondering what's become of us,' he said, and turning he began to climb the zigzag path.

'Frank,' I called after him, 'are you right happy about having Wint Craig on our pay-roll?' Carlos, standing next to me, seemed as anxious to hear my brother's reply as I was.

Frank's voice came low. 'Just remember, Jim, you weren't here and I wasn't figuring on you showing up. We had a whole lot of trouble on our hands and things came to a head. Pa's killing was only a part of it. Them sheepherders is mighty strong — a lot of trigger-happy young bloods. I needed somebody around who wasn't scared of them; somebody to help me drive them out, and to nail the man responsible for Pa's death. Can't you see that?'

'I thought Craig got ten years in the pen?' I said.

Frank shrugged his shoulders impatiently. 'A man don't ask questions when he needs help as bad as I did.'

After a while I said, 'Okay, Frank. If Craig proves hisself honourable, I guess we can do with his help.'

The tension seemed to flow out of Frank, and just for a second he smiled. 'I knew you'd see it my way, Jim. Come on, let's head back for the Double Horseshoe.'

We toiled up the gulley side, and

58

Frank reached the top first. I saw him suddenly stiffen. Joining him, Carlos and I could see Mattie racing through the rocks towards us, scrambling as though the Devil was chasing her. We moved down the slope to meet her.

'Riders!' she gasped. 'I saw 'em through the trees.'

Frank reached out and steadied her. 'Who were they?'

'Sheepherders — a whole bunch of 'em. And they've spotted us for sure!'

5

From way back in the cottonwoods where we'd left the horses, came Copper's spooked whinny, and we could hear the scrambling progress of men ripping their way through the foliage.

Frank drew his gun, thumbing lead into place. 'They've got our horses, damn them!'

Without warning, a single shot rang out and grit and earth spat down about us. I dragged Mattie to the ground behind the scant rock cover. Frank and Carlos were sprawled belly-flat, their eyes combing the trees for sign of the hidden marksman. A bullet had ploughed into the bank, just a few inches above where my head had been. Again the high-pitched whinny of Copper lifted into the hush which had followed the gunshot.

Responding instantly to a slight movement in the bushes below us, Frank shattered the silence with a rapid succession of shots, but there came no sound to indicate if he'd found a mark.

I forced Mattie further down into the rocks and unholstered my own Colt. I hadn't figured on using this so soon when I'd strapped it on. I wondered if Pa's killer was down there in the trees, and anger cut through me.

'Wagh! This time they've caught us with our pants down!' Carlos growled.

'They've got us treed,' Frank muttered, 'and they know we'll damn well keep. They ain't in no hurry.'

Sure enough we were in a mess, flattened behind the scant cover. The trees provided more than sufficient cover for our enemies, and having captured our horses, they were holding all the aces.

Four quick rifle-shots had us ducking, and lead ricocheted amid the rocks. A brief silence, then a single shot cracked out, the bullet thudding into the ground uncomfortably close. But this time the orange stab of flame had shown clear against the greenery of the trees. Our three guns exploded almost simultaneously, splintering the bark of the trees around the spot where the shot had come from. We strained to hear the giveaway howl that somebody was hit, but it didn't come.

There were plenty of other noises though, sounds of movement in the timber. We couldn't see anybody, but it sounded as if a whole army was laying siege.

Again flame stabbed out of the greenery, but this time from several places. I lay across Mattie so heavily that it was a wonder she was able to breathe.

Then the shooting died out once more, and Frank's grit-hard voice came: 'The bastards sure ain't funnin'!'

'I wish they'd show themselves a leetle bit,' muttered Carlos, pulling off his sombrero and peering gingerly over his meagre cover.

Mattie lay very quiet and still. I eased my weight clear of her. 'How many of them did you see?' I asked.

Her face was grimed from burrowing in the dirt. 'I think about eight.'

'Did you recognize any of them?' queried Frank.

'N-no,' she came back uncertainly, 'just knew they were sheepherders.' After a glance at me, she added, 'Sam Crevis was among them — couldn't mistake him.'

Crevis! A red blaze of hate hovered before my eyes. I leapt up from cover and fired wildly into the trees, thoughts of Janet cradled in Crevis's arms blinding me to danger. Then a rifle cracked from below, its bullet passing so close that its lethal breath fanned my cheek.

Mattie dragged me down, screaming at me not to be a fool. I knew I'd acted stupidly, but these damned sheepherders had killed my father, taken my woman and even grabbed my horse — and now it looked as though they were all set to finish off the rest of the Bannerman family. But maybe we weren't licked yet. The plan that was shaping in my mind was desperate, but anything was better than waiting to be picked off one by one.

'Frank!' I hissed, but as he looked around the blast of rifle-fire sounded, forcing us to duck down. I realized that Carlos was cursing. He'd sagged back against the rock, his hand clutching his shoulder as blood streamed through his fingers.

'Just a scratch,' he said through gritted teeth.

I made up my mind. Carlos's 'scratch' had already soaked his shirt-front with blood. Unless we made our move pretty soon, it would be too late.

I ripped the calico bandanna from my neck and gestured for Frank and Mattie to do likewise. Mattie then tied the three together, fashioning a crude bandage.

'If I can get up the bank behind us,' I said, 'and into the gulley, I could get round behind them. Maybe then, I could scare them off and get to the horses.'

'You'll never get over that bank, Meester Jim. It'll be suicide!' Carlos's mouth was sagging beneath the sweat-limp curl of his moustache.

Frank looked up the slope behind us. Those ten yards to the ridge were really exposed, but right now it seemed our only chance. Turning back, he grunted his agreement. 'You're right, Jim. It might be possible.'

Mattie was about to plead with me not to try it, but before she could say anything, I hissed, 'Get Carlos bandaged afore he bleeds to death!'

She went to work, ripping Carlos's shirt open to reveal an ugly wound in his left shoulder. She managed to staunch the flow of blood and manipulate the makeshift bandage into place. Meanwhile I reloaded my Colt.

'Frank,' I cried, 'give me covering fire!'

Then I scrambled furiously upwards.

In my desperation I slipped on the loose soil, but somehow I clung on, clawing at the ground and pushing out with my legs. Behind me all hell was let loose. Bullets were buzzing around my head. I was briefly aware of the inadequate snap of Frank's and Carlos's covering fire, but this seemed drowned out by the roar of the sheepherders' rifles. I zigzagged frenziedly in order to present as elusive a target as possible; lead splattered about me, throwing up sharp splinters of rock.

Suddenly the ridge loomed ahead of me, but as I straightened to hurl myself across it, something rammed into my back. The whole world seemed to twist before me as I shot forward, conscious that my feet were no longer in contact with the ground. The split second I was in the air seemed an eternity, then with the earth leaping at my face I threw up my arms for protection. I wasn't quick enough; my head cracked against the sun-hardened crust and from then on things became hazed.

Somehow my eyes registered that my hat was rolling downwards in front of me, bouncing on the rocks but not stopping. Just as I imagined it would never stop, it struck a large rock and bounced across the strip of sand onto the slow-moving surface of the river.

I realized I'd made it. I was in the gulley! Relief cut through me, clearing my senses and filling me with new determination.

Behind me the sound of gunfire was muffled by the hump of the hill. I figured I must have been pretty badly hit. I gingerly moved, expecting to feel crippling pains across my back. But I felt nothing more serious than the all-over pain of the battering I'd taken. Reaching round behind me, I felt the soggy wetness of my shirt, but withdrawing my hand I saw no sign of blood — just wholesome sweat. It must have been a large lump of bullet-thrown sod that had knocked me flying.

Luck had been with me, and now I had to make the best of that luck. Every second's delay increased the sheepherders' chances of gunning down Frank, Mattie or Carlos. Having seen me being rammed over the ridge, everyone would most likely figure me a dead man, which gave me an advantage.

Scrambling to my feet, I slithered down into the soft sand of the gulley. Ahead of me a great bluff rose out of the water; there was no chance of getting over its top, so I unbuckled my gunbelt, slung it around my neck and for the second time that day waded into the river. The bottom cut away sharply beneath my feet, forcing me to rely on the weeds that grew out of the rock-face to pull my way along.

For five minutes I struggled on, often slipping. My arms ached from the strain of supporting my weight. At last the river shallowed and I felt its firm bed beneath me. I found a groove in the rock about three feet above the surface, got both hands into it and hauled upwards. My knees got purchase in the groove, then my boot, and soon I was around the bluff. Meanwhile, the barrage of gunfire had continued unbroken.

Another couple of minutes hard climbing saw the hillside dipping down in front of me, cloaked in the tangled brush which reached out towards the cottonwoods. I strapped my gunbelt back where it belonged, unholstered my gun, and weighed up my chances. Way off to the left, on the fringe of the timber, I spotted a group of horses, but they weren't our animals. There was no sign of life in my immediate vicinity, though there was plenty of noise coming from the trees.

Clutching my gun, I charged my way through the brush, reached the shadow of the timber and flung myself down.

I could hear somebody blundering through the foliage close by. Up ahead guns were still firing, while from not far in front of me came the sound of horses shifting nervously — no doubt Copper and our other animals.

I had no clearly defined plan; I knew only that my kin were well-nigh finished up there on the hillside, and their one slim hope of survival lay in my luck holding.

Having got my breath back, I stood up, ripped aside the branches and ran forward into a clearing. A sideways glance registered a scurry of wheeling chestnut, and then came Copper's welcoming nicker. I swung back — and blundered head-on into a sheepherder! In that fleeting second, I glimpsed a sweating face, bulging eyes and sagging mouth, then I lashed out with the barrel of my Colt. I connected solidly with the side of his skull and he crumpled. As I stumbled on, a fresh figure barged into my path. My gun jerked upwards, but as I pressed the trigger recognition came and I swung the weapon off-target and the bullet blazed harmlessly through the air. I struck out with my left arm, catching the man a glancing blow across the side of his neck and he went spinning away through the bush. I'd been within a hair's-breadth of killing Janet's brother, Nat Shaughnessy!

The situation now took a surprising twist. There was still plenty of firing, but no longer from up ahead. It was coming from off to the left, beyond the trees. Suddenly I heard the pounding of hooves. 'Let's get the hell outa here!' somebody yelled, and men were rushing through the trees on every side.

I spun round, spotted Copper, and took a running leap into the saddle. We were lunging forward as I rammed my toes into the stirrups — and that was when Sam Crevis burst into the clearing!

I had a quick glimpse of his rugged features glancing at me before Copper ran him down. The chestnut staggered and I ducked to avoid being clawed from his back by low-hanging branches, then we were racing onward.

Copper had carried me out of the timber before I was able to halt him. For a second I just sat there dazzled by the sun's brightness and aware that some new influence had turned the tide of battle. I gazed up the slope and saw Frank running towards me, with Mattie helping the wounded Carlos along not far behind.

I nudged Copper towards them, and as Mattie pointed I saw on our right riders spurring their mounts into the timber-fringe. The snap of their six-shooters had replaced the deeper cadence of rifle-fire. They were the men of the Double Horseshoe.

As Frank reached me, he clasped my saddle-horn for support. 'Thank God Wint Craig showed up,' he panted.

Mattie had stumbled in now, and she hugged onto my hand. 'And thank God Jim's all right,' she gasped. 'When we saw you fall, we thought . . . '

Carlos, still clutching his shoulder, was grinning broadly. 'It was like the old days, Meester Jim, when Señor

Bannerman and I were fighting the Utes!'

I laughed. Suddenly I remembered Sam Crevis. Had Copper's hooves pounded him to death? Dismounting, I pressed the reins into Mattie's hands. 'Hold these for me. I won't be long.' Before she could respond, I'd turned and was running down the slope into the trees.

All firing had now ceased; I could hear horses moving into the open behind me. Soon I was in the clearing, searching for the crushed remains of Sam Crevis. All I found was flattened brush. Cursing, I had to admit that right now Crevis must be thundering away from Peakman's Gulley astride a Double Horseshoe animal.

In disgust, I rejoined Frank and the others just as the Double Horseshoe riders were halting their horses around them. I saw the big Texan Ben Wells, and acknowledged his greeting. There were ten others, and I searched their faces to see if I knew any of them,

73

but all were strangers: typical drifting cowboys who most likely intended staying in Double Horseshoe employ only until the fall round-up. But today they were on our side and they'd arrived at a mighty opportune moment.

'Where did Wint get to?' demanded a narrow-shouldered little cowboy who had reined in close to Frank. As he looked about him I noticed he had an eye missing, leaving a sunken socket, red-slitted and ugly.

The answer was fast coming, the voice deep and arrogant. 'I guess I'm right here, One-Eye!'

All eyes turned down-slope. Wint Craig edged his bay horse clear of the trees and sat there for a moment, his lank, rangy body lithe and erect in his saddle. His thin-lipped grin was as cold and hard as deep-winter ice. I felt the old uneasiness clawing at my belly muscles. It always came when his gaze flicked over me.

He wheeled his horse slightly, and it was then that we saw he was gripping the end of his lariat. He jerked on the rope and with a vicious heave dragged a dishevelled figure out of the trees. The cringing captive was Silas Wade, the sheepherder I'd collided with in the clearing and laid out with the barrel of my gun.

Craig slipped one of his ivory-butted Colts from its holster. 'Reckon we'll have one bastard less!' His voice was mad. Wade turned dazed, pleading eyes upward, a cry for mercy forming on his lips. Craig's gun belched flame. Wade was blasted off his feet, his face transformed to a grotesque, bloody pulp . . .

Mattie screamed, burying her face in Frank's shirt-front. Minutes before, I'd been prepared to kill — but not like this. This was stark, cold-blooded murder!

Frank's voice sounded strangely loud in the shocked silence. 'Come on, boys. Let's make tracks.'

I caught hold of Mattie; her face pale. I mounted Copper and helped her up in front of me. Frank and Carlos were also riding double with a couple of other men. As we moved out, I saw Craig flicking his rope clear of Wade's corpse before he fell in behind us.

6

We reined in our horses in the yard fronting the Double Horseshoe and dismounting I lifted Mattie down. She'd had a rough time, and yet even now, as I gestured for her to go into the house and take a rest, she pushed my arm aside and went over to Carlos. He was looking mighty seedy and his left arm was hanging limp. With Mattie steadying him, he walked slowly towards his cabin.

Maria, heavy with child, appeared in the cabin doorway, gasping in alarm as she saw her husband.

Knowing Carlos was now in good hands, I slackened Copper's cinches and was turning him towards the stable when I sensed somebody was watching me. I swung round and met Wint Craig's staring eyes. He was lounging against his bay horse, an insolent grin tugging at his lips. He spat out a stalk of grass he'd been chewing on, then laughed his humourless, near-silent laugh.

'Seems we're on the same side of the fence now, Mister Bannerman,' he said. His expression hardened and his voice came menacingly low: 'I've waited one hell of a while to get myself on your side of the fence!' He pivoted on his heel and led his horse away.

I stood there, chilled by his malevolent words. Sure enough he'd got us out of a bad scrape that day, but it was doubtful that his motives were governed by any real concern for the Bannermans. But why had he done it? Of one thing I was becoming increasingly sure: say what he might, Frank had made a grave mistake in taking Wint Craig into employ.

That night I couldn't sleep. I mentally relived the day, vainly seeking answers to a hundred questions. Eventually, I got up. I struck a match and held it to my clock. 2 a.m. The flame illuminated the photograph of

Janet on the dresser. Even in the faint light I could see the gentle lines of her face and her boyish smile.

I figured I might sleep if I bedded down in the open. I left the house and climbed a knoll. I lay back gazing up at the stars, recalling the way Frank had been at the dance those three years back. He'd changed now. He was harder and unyielding. Had Janet also changed? I told myself she hadn't — time would prove she was the same. The thought soothed me; I drifted into sleep.

I awoke to see the pale sky of dawn.

★ ★ ★

A few hours later, sipping Maria's wine, I was relieved to see Carlos looking more like his old self. His arm was in a sling. 'Maria and her Ute remedies!' he grinned. 'They work so well, I can't even complain.'

Maria bustled in with a platter of

steaming cakes. Her time was near but she still kept busy.

As we ploughed into the cookies, I said to Carlos, 'I'm going into Coltville today. I want to have a word with Marshal Dainton.'

'He's useless, Meester Jim,' Carlos scoffed.

We looked up as Frank walked in through the door. He tossed his hat aside and sat down. 'Won't be long now,' he announced. 'Wint Craig's got some of his pals riding in next week. We'll be strong enough then. We'll cross the river and finish the sheepherders for good!'

I winced at the thought. 'What're you paying Craig?'

'Plenty,' Frank snapped. 'It's worth every cent!'

'I suppose you think murdering innocent folk'll avenge Pa's death.'

He came to his feet angrily. 'You're damned right. Figured on more support from you, though!'

'Craig ain't nothing but a butcher,'

I got out. 'He'll kill for pleasure or profit, and he'd as soon put a slug in our backs as anyone else's.'

His eyes blazing fury, Frank stamped out.

Carlos sighed. 'It is not good that you two fight.'

I drained the wine from my cup. 'I'm gonna visit this marshal in Coltville — see what I can find out.' I thanked Maria for her kindness, then stepped out.

Carlos joined me. 'I'll get the horses.'

'Why, you can't come, Carlos,' I told him. 'Not shot up the way you are.'

'A man needs only this hand to shoot.' His right hand slapped his Colt.

'You're a game varmint!' I laughed as we saddled up.

We were passing the house when I heard Frank call. I saw him standing on the verandah. I rode over to him, feeling uneasy, not liking the rift that had come between us — but the old, sudden switch of his manner was there to surprise me. It was as if the incident of a few minutes before had never occurred.

'I've been thinking, Jim,' he said quietly. 'I feel bad about you having been dragged back into all this trouble. Mattie should've let things settle. You know, when we were kids you used to say you just weren't suited to ranch life — maybe there was something to that.'

My boyhood dreams had led me to do a lot of grand talking, but much had happened since then.

Frank was picking his words carefully. 'I guess we don't agree about plenty, Jim, but I won't rest till the sheep-herders are driven out. Pa would want that.'

Pa would never have used outlaws and killers to achieve his aims, but I left the thought unspoken.

'Look, Jim,' he went on, 'why not sell your share of the ranch to me? I'll give you a fair price, then you'll be free to go make that fortune you dreamed about. Just chew it over before you make up your mind definite.'

He turned and walked back into the house.

As Carlos and I rode out of the ranch, I was angry. Why did Frank suddenly want me out of it? He'd seemed glad enough to have me around when I'd first got back.

Then, as usual, I found myself looking at things through his eyes. After all, he'd lived in Grand Valley these last few years, whereas I hadn't, and it was clear that he'd have the better knowledge of how much the law could be relied upon — which seemed just about nil. But I knew that even when peace at last returned to Grand Valley, I would never sell out. I belonged here just as much as Pa had done, and just as much as Frank himself.

After an hour's ride we reached the outflanks of Coltville, passing the familiar building of the schoolhouse with its great bell set church-like on the roof.

Further on, past some log cabins, we drew abreast of the grand, white building that was the house of Hilda Zimm. It stood alone and ludicrously out of place on the town's outskirts. In the early days, this house had only one meaning to the local townsfolk; it had been the home of Milly Zimm, a lady of decidedly easy virtue, who had gleaned enough from the pockets of wandering cowboys, night-furtive local gentry, and many others, to turn her strange house into something approaching a palace. The house was filled with fancy trinkets and ornaments which Milly seemed to love above all else in the world.

But five years back, Milly had died. The fact that Hilda, her young and beautiful daughter, had continued to live alone, had set tongues wagging. Rumours still flourished, but whatever was said, no proof was ever brought to light that Hilda was the same 'professional woman' as her mother was. Yet fuel was added to the gossip by the fact that she had no visible means of support through other sources. Hilda, as I knew full well, was Frank's girl, and he would have killed anybody who as much as hinted that she was a whore.

The house, surrounded by its low wooden fence, was set back from the trail. I watched the doorway as we drew level, wondering if Hilda might appear. Sure enough, she stepped out onto the verandah, a graceful figure in an elegant eastern-style dress. Her hair was the colour of burnished gold. She lifted a hand, shading her eyes against the sun, to see who we were.

'That one ees all woman,' Carlos muttered.

I nodded, swinging Copper off-trail towards her. I figured it was only right to pass the time of day. I gave her a wave, and it was then she recognized me because she stiffened, and, for some reason, hurriedly turned and disappeared into the house, closing the door.

I reined in, amazed and sore at being

treated so. 'What the hell's eating her?' I asked Carlos.

He said just one word, shaking his head. 'Women!'

We swung our horses back onto the trail. Five minutes later we rode into town and hitched our animals to the rail outside the marshal's office. Across the street was the red-painted front of 'The Bull Fly' saloon, and from its interior came the sound of loud voices and the tinkle of a piano. Carlos glanced apprehensively at the four horses hitched outside the saloon, then relaxed. 'No sheepherders in town, Meester Jim. Still, I'll wait right here and keep my eyes open.'

I nodded my thanks and made my way up the steps and into the marshal's office.

Gregg Miller was in the outer office cleaning his gun. Seeing me enter, he set the gun on the table and stood up, his good-looking face creased with a smile. 'Hell, if it ain't Jim Bannerman!' He reached out and shook my hand. Miller, a six-footer, had broad shoulders, a thatch of blond hair and a grin which displayed white teeth. The old reckless devil-may-care glint still showed in his eyes, albeit somewhat subdued.

His grin faded. 'Sure is good to see you, Jim. But I guess it ain't been much of a happy homecoming.'

'No, Gregg,' I admitted. 'But right now I want to know what the law's doing to find out who killed Pa. Is Marshal Dainton around?' I glanced towards the half-open door of the inner office.

'He's gone across the street to get something to eat,' Gregg explained. 'Won't be long, though.'

He gestured me into a chair and sat down himself. Looking over his shoulder, I could see that the two cells stood open and empty. 'What sort of fella is Jim Dainton?' I asked. 'What's it like being his deputy?'

He scowled. 'He's useless, Jim. After Harry Bouchel went, folks were mighty desperate for a new man. I'd figured I was gonna step in, but just at that time I got myself throwed off my hoss. Busted up my right wrist. It looked like I was finished with gun-play for good, and right then Dainton rides in, along with a fair old reputation from Kansas City — God knows how he did it — and he got the job. Anyway, Jim, it was weeks before I could even hold a gun, but in time my wrist healed up better'n I ever dreamed — and here I am, back as deputy.'

'What's Dainton done to find Pa's killer?' I asked.

He started to reply, but stopped. 'Here he comes.'

The outside door opened, and I swung round and got my first look at Town Marshal Jim Dainton. His Strauss jacket lolled open to hang either side of a bulging paunch, and the rest of him was podgy and thick-set to match. His eyes were toad-like and expressionless.

'This here's Jim Bannerman,' Gregg

introduced. 'He's Frank's brother.'

'I've come to find out what the law's doing to bring order to the valley,' I said.

'Does Frank know you're here?' Dainton enquired.

'Maybe.'

'Come in here.' He nodded towards the inner office. As we went in he made a point of closing the door behind me, clearly not wanting Gregg to hear what was going on. He sank his hulk into a chair behind his desk, took a cigar from a box and lit up. He opened a drawer, brought out a glass and poured himself a stiff tot of liquor. He didn't offer me any. I was getting impatient.

'I don't have all day,' I said.

He drew on his cigar, then placed it in an ash-tray. 'When your father got killed, your brother and me made a thorough search. I went up to the sheepherders' cabins, but there was nothing to throw any light on the killing. There's a lot of wandering cowboys and badmen passing through

Grand Valley, sonny. They come and they go; nobody keeps track of them. Seems to me that one of them was responsible for shooting your pa. That being so, there ain't a blamed thing that can be done — 'cept keeping a watch out for strangers around, of course.'

'Damnfool yarn that is,' I shouted. 'There's enough fighting and feuding in this valley to blow it apart. And you give me a lot of drivel about passing strangers!'

His drawer was open again, with his hand inside. I suspected that his fat fingers were caressing a pistol.

'Sure there's friction,' he said, 'private friction. Frank nor nobody else'd want the law poking into that!'

'Dainton,' I said angrily, 'if you've not got the guts to do something about an honest man's murder, it's time the county sheriff was brought here from Dalton.'

Dainton jerked to his feet. For the first time there was emotion in his eyes. 'There'd be certain elements in Coltville,' he spat out, 'that'd be against any such action, sonny . . . very much against it!'

Had I stayed there any longer, I'd have grabbed his fat neck; instead I stamped out, slamming the door.

Gregg Miller looked at me, shaking his blond head.

I needed a strong whiskey. 'I'm going to wash a bad taste out of my mouth,' I said. 'You coming, Gregg?'

He nodded and followed me outside. Carlos looked at me enquiringly, then seeing my expression, didn't bother to speak. Crossing the street, we entered 'The Bull Fly' saloon. We set ourselves up with liquor.

'Let's sit,' Gregg suggested, picking up the bottle. We found a table and sat down. Carlos remained just inside the batwings, so he could see into the street. He didn't intend any sheepherders to catch us unawares.

I poured myself a drink. In the corner, the piano continued its monotonous jangling. The only other customers were some cowboys, crowded around one of the poker-tables. They unleashed bursts of ribald laughter and noisy jibing. From behind the bar, the barman looked on with bored indifference; above him from the huge painting, a big-breasted lady smiled down complacently.

'This whole damned business makes me sick,' Gregg said, 'but I'm hamstrung, Jim. If I go against Dainton, I'll be out of a job, and I ain't hankering to lose it.'

'Do you want to lose Mattie, Gregg?'

'Mattie!' His cheeks coloured. 'If only she'd let me speak to her.' His eyes met mine and I felt real sorry for him. 'Believe me, Jim, I love Mattie. If she'd let me see her, mebbe I could explain that our only chance of getting a good living is for me to swallow my disgust at the way things are being run. One day, sure as oats, I'll be marshal. Things'll change then, Jim. I can promise that. Will you try to make her understand?'

I drained my glass. 'I'll do my best, Gregg.' I stood up. 'Better be getting back, I guess.'

Right then there was a sudden commotion behind me. Carlos's alarmed voice had the piano trailing to a halt.

'Wagon just pulled into the street, Meester Jim. Brack Shaughnessy's in eet — and Janet!'

7

Gregg said something and his arm came across my chest. I brushed it aside and walked towards the batwings. Carlos was talking quickly, warningly, but his words had no meaning in my ears. I knew only that Janet was close at hand, and come hell or high water I had to see her.

A light spring-board wagon was drawn up against the sidewalk a few yards down on the opposite side of the street. My mind barely registered the fact that a man had stepped from it and moved into the gunsmith's nearby.

She was sitting quietly in the wagon waiting her brother's return, slender hands pressed into her lap, as cool and as pretty in all that afternoon heat as the first flower of spring. Her dress was of white calico, and beneath a small bonnet the swirl of her hair was drawn back and tied with yellow ribbon, half revealing the whiteness of her neck.

All the old emotion welled up within me. I was through the batwings of the saloon, across the street and standing doe-eyed and foolish when she turned her head. Suddenly I was gazing into those green-grey eyes which had haunted me since childhood.

'Jim . . . ' The voice came in the softest of surprised whispers, yet to me it held all the power of a mountain torrent. She leaned towards me, thin calico pulled tight across her breasts. For those brief, wildly exciting moments her lips were scarcely inches from mine, and the urge was in me to reach up and take her in my arms. Then I felt the tentative, almost unbelieving touch of her fingers on my face. I lifted my hand and hers came readily into it, clinging tightly.

'Janet,' I gasped, 'is it true . . . ?'

'Take your filthy hands off my sister!'

I turned at the sound of Brack

Shaughnessy's harsh voice. He stepped stiff-legged from the sidewalk.

'Bannerman,' he snarled, 'I'm gonna kill you!'

With Janet's scream of 'No, Brack!' ringing in my ears, I recalled Carlos's tense warning as I'd come through those batwings. *He's fast with a gun, that one!*

I edged clear of Janet, aware that she was sitting bolt upright, her face drained of all colour.

Brack Shaughnessy moved round the horses, the radiated fingers of his right hand poised above the low-slung Colt at his hip, an arrogant grin on his lips.

'Go for your gun, Bannerman,' he said.

I could feel eyes turned upon us from the sidewalk. There was a scurrying to get clear of the line of fire.

I edged backwards, knowing that the slightest false move would have Shaughnessy's hand flashing down. It was three years since I'd tested the speed of my draw. I knew I wouldn't stand a chance against Brack.

'I'm telling you for the last time!' His voice had risen almost to a scream. '*Go for your gun!*'

For five seconds we stood there, motionless, the sweat of fear trickling down inside my shirt. Then I found my voice. 'You might put a bullet in me, Brack, but if you take a look on the verandah outside 'The Bull Fly', you'll realize that before I hit the dirt, you'll be as dead as your own mutton!'

It was a long shot, and it paid off. The sound of Gregg Miller clicking back the hammer of his Colt was like music in my ears. I saw Brack's eyes flicker, uncertainty replacing his confidence, yet it seemed an eternity before he finally backed down. Wordlessly he stepped over to the wagon, climbed aboard and rein-whipped his horses into motion. I had one last glimpse of Janet's white face glancing back as the dust clouded, then the wagon gathered speed and seconds later was gone.

The street came suddenly to life. People popped out from doorways and emerged from behind water-troughs. Anxious mothers released the hands of their children, men turned back to drinking.

Maybe I deserved a bullet that day, for the blind, pigheaded way I'd blundered into near disaster. I looked round into the serious faces of Gregg and Carlos — but Gregg suddenly grinned. 'Reckon we need another drink, Jim,' and we moved back into the saloon.

But right then I wasn't really thinking about whiskey, or even Brack Shaughnessy. I was recalling that three years had made Janet even more beautiful and downright desirable. I swore to myself that no matter what else happened in Grand Valley, I would make her mine.

Carlos was anxious to leave Coltville in case more sheepherders showed up. It wasn't long before we had taken our leave of Gregg and were riding out of town.

The heat was oppressive as we rode, and a deathly quietness lay over the land. Carlos glanced upward. Storm-clouds were sweeping in from the west and the brightness had gone out of the sky. As the first rumble of thunder broke the silence, he muttered 'Soon we will be in for a drenching, Meester Jim.'

He was riding hunched forward in his saddle, and he looked tired. I knew his wound was paining him. The threat of impending rain deepened my feeling of depression. We were not one step further towards finding out who'd killed Pa, and all I'd achieved, for all my high ideas, was to make myself more enemies.

Lightning forked the heavens and thunder rumbled, louder and closer. The light was fading fast as big raindrops began to fall. We pulled on our slickers and spurred our animals, anxious to reach the ranch.

We'd barely made another two miles when a movement on the hillside to the north drew my attention. I yelled into the rising wind for Carlos to pull up, then pointed towards the hills. Straining our eyes into the dim light, we spotted a lone horseman. The erratic swerving of his horse could only mean that the rider was in trouble.

'Come on, Carlos,' I shouted, 'we'll cut his trail!'

The rider was slanting in ahead of us. I spurred Copper and his powerful stride lengthened into a belly-flat gallop. Above our heads the thunder crashed out again.

It was obvious that the oncoming horse was completely out of control. The rider was swaying drunkenly; and there was something familiar about the broad set of his shoulders. The horse hit a patch of rough ground about a hundred yards before our trails converged — and then the inevitable happened. The rider was jerked from his saddle, hitting the ground heavily. One foot remained hooked in its stirrup, and for twenty yards he was dragged over the rugged prairie. Then the horse went down in a flurry of blood-flecked foam and flailing hooves. The animal was sprawled there, trembling and ruined, as I halted Copper alongside.

Pinned beneath the tortured animal I found straw-haired Ben Wells, foreman of the Double Horseshoe. He was crying out in agony as I dismounted, his face caked with blood and dirt. The horse was struggling with its forelegs in a hopeless effort to rise. Each jerk of its weight brought fresh agony to Wells.

I drew my gun, sliding its barrel beneath the animal's ear. The shot was almost drowned out by the renewed rumble of thunder.

Carlos pounded up, cursing savagely at what he saw. Together we dragged the dead weight of the horse clear of the man, Carlos straining with his one good arm.

The fact that Ben Wells still survived was amazing; the sight of him was sickening. His body was crushed, his clothes no more than blood-sodden rags, and there were powder-blackened edges to the gaping hole in his chest where a shot had been fired into him.

His staring eyes flickered with recognition and he struggled to say something, but only frothy blood bubbled from between his lips. I raised the Texan's head and Carlos laid a canteen to his mouth. Water trickled down his chin, but a little of it must have seeped into his mouth because he coughed and looked up at me. He was nearly gone, but with extreme effort he moved his lips to speak. I held my ear close, barely catching his dying words . . . 'They . . . they hit us on the Coyote Lake range . . . got the cattle . . . Tom Glint and Symes, both dead.'

The rain was driving down as the Texan died. Carlos went over and stood bowed against his horse.

Presently, I laid the body of Ben Wells back onto the ground. I came to my feet, weary, sick and cold. I walked across to Carlos.

'Go back,' I said, lifting my voice into the wind. 'Tell my brother what's happened. I'm going after the cattle. Tell Frank to follow me up as soon as possible.'

8

With Ben Wells's last words still echoing in my ears, I urged my horse through the rain. The brush and grass was flattened in the blind rush of the gale. I was forcing Copper on as I'd never done before.

Coyote Lake range consisted of the flats sprawling between the southward curve of the Smoke Mountains and the lake-broadened section of the Ute River. It was the main summer grazing-ground of the Double Horseshoe. Here it was that Frank had put our finest Hereford beef-herd to fatten on the choice verdure, ready for round-up and the drive to the rail-heads in the fall. Two hundred head of the best stock the Double Horseshoe had ever raised, and all but ready for market. Frank had miscalculated that its remoteness would make it safe.

Ben Wells had suffered agony before death claimed him, and yet his only thought had been to get word back to the ranch of the attack. The Double Horseshoe had lost a loyal servant. I hadn't known the Texan for long, but all at once I felt as if one of my closest friends had departed. Apache Tom Glint and ex-cavalryman Hank Symes were undoubtedly good men as well.

They hit us on Coyote Lake range! Who were the *they* Wells had spoken of? The memory of thirty sheep carcasses and the sure lust for revenge left no doubt.

Two hours later, I gave Copper an overdue rest. I'd made it to Coyote Lake range, with not the slightest let-up in the downpour. Somewhere ahead of me, I knew, would be the prone bodies of Glint and Symes, yet it would be futile to attempt to trace them in the gloom.

Dismounting, I stood in the lee of my horse. The wind was a crazy thing about me, howling and shrieking. In the fleeting brilliance of the lightning, the surrounding land seemed unreal and hideous.

I tried to figure which way I'd have headed had I been in those rustlers' boots. I reckoned they must have put the cattle across the narrow strip of the Ute River which separated the two great lakes of the flats.

I mounted up again, and presently the storm-whipped whiteness of water showed ahead; I'd hit the first of the lakes. I rode on the shingle close to the water. At last the lake was narrowing beside me, and I reached the point where the cattle had in all probability been driven across. But the river was now swollen, its swirling surface ugly and black.

About eight miles up-river there had once been a bridge. For a while I debated whether I should ride on and see if the bridge was still crossable, or force Copper into the river here and attempt to swim it. In the back of my mind was the notion that if only I could get sight of the herd, I might be able to do some good — though just how, I hadn't the faintest idea as yet.

I wondered if Frank was following me up, and if so, how far behind he was.

I made up my mind quite suddenly. I'd do the crossing here. Slipping my rifle from its saddle-scabbard, I raised it high and kneed my reluctant mount into the uninviting swirl of the river. This was the biggest mistake I could have made!

Copper's terrified whinny lifted into the gale as the water took command of us. We were puny toys in its mighty grip. Copper's legs were swept from under him, and he was pitched right over in panicking, threshing confusion. Like a fly, I clung to his back, my rifle having dropped from my grasp. I fought desperately to bring Copper the right way up, but I was handicapped by my clothes which were sodden and heavy. Near paralysed with cold, I lost my hold on him and I went over sideways, plunging down into blackness, water gushing into my mouth. A stab of pain as my knee struck bottom, then I was struggling upwards, fighting for my life. I broke surface and helplessly surrendered myself to the current, striving desperately to locate Copper's bobbing hulk in the seething torrent — but there was nothing.

The river was thick with churned-up debris, uprooted trees and bushes. My only hope was to strike a sand-bar or be driven close enough to the shore further down so I could reach up and grasp the overhanging tree branches. Several times I was dragged under in the mad rush of the current, only to struggle to the surface again gasping for breath, and all the while I was being drawn on and on with increasing power. All count of time and all reasoning of distance were lost to me. And then I became aware of a new sound — the deeper roar of rapids ahead!

Through the spray, I glimpsed the

up-jut of rocks drawing nearer, white foam crashing around and over them. The noise had risen to a deafening crescendo. They say a drowning man's life passes before him in the final moments — that's probably why Janet somehow got herself entangled in my thoughts. Hell, I'd have given anything to have got out of this alive, and been able to prove that there was nothing between her and Sam Crevis . . .

Branches clawed at my face, and staring wildly into the darkness I saw the black outline of a thick bough reaching out over the water like a giant arm. Summoning all my remaining strength, I made a life-or-death grab.

The jerk of my sudden halt near broke my neck.

★ ★ ★

For three miserable hours that night, I combed through the trees lining the river, hoping that Copper might loom out of the rain, nickering forgiveness at the shoddy way I'd treated him. At last I made my way back to the shore directly opposite the point where I'd started my ill-fated crossing, and straining my eyes I sought the outline of a patiently waiting horse, but then I realized how futile it was. I had to get used to the idea. My gallant chestnut was long gone by now, his dead hulk smashed by the rocks.

For half the night I crouched beneath the trees, feeling utterly wretched. There seemed no end to my troubles. At the bottom of the river, along with my horse, were my rifle and pistol, and I was soaked and frozen and stranded in the wildest country God ever created — and where was Frank?

Despite the wet and cold, I eventually dozed. I had no idea for how long I slept, but suddenly I jolted into wakefulness. I climbed to my feet, stiff and aching. I worked my limbs to restore the circulation.

The rain had ceased, though it was still dark. Stripping myself, I wrung out my clothes as best I could. Shivering, I restored my clothes, then struck southwards through the timber. Somewhere ahead was the old Spanish trail through the Mescalero Mountains — and also ahead of me, I figured, were two hundred head of Double Horseshoe Herefords being driven for the Mexican line.

I maintained a steady dog-trot until dawn, when I took a much-needed rest. In the misty morning light, the rearing peaks of mountains were visible above the trees. It took me another hour to reach the Spanish trail, and by then the sun's warmth had dried much of the dampness from my clothes and brought a lift to my sagging spirits.

Presently I found sign of the stolen herd — rain-sodden droppings and hoof-marks. My hunch had paid off, but I reckoned the cattle were still way ahead of me.

I was dead tired and well-nigh starving, but realization that with each passing minute the herd was getting nearer the Mexican border, had me quickening my pace. The trail widened before me, lifting and twisting towards the mountains. On each side, rocky hills cut back, thickly timbered; here everything was green and fresh, the air full of squirrel-chatter, the cheery, drawn-out calls of quail and the rasp of crickets.

I still hoped that Frank and the Double Horseshoe riders might be between me and the cattle, but as the hours slipped by that prospect diminished.

In the early afternoon, creased with weariness, I threw myself down at the side of the trail. A half-hour later, my rumbling belly could no longer be ignored, and finding some edible berries, I began to eat them. It was then I heard the thump of hooves approaching from beyond a bend in the trail. I dodged down in the brush.

A solitary horseman came into view, mud-caked from a long ride. He reined-in just a few yards from where I was hidden. He fumbled with the makings of a smoke. I realized it was Tom Crevis, Sam's younger brother.

He was jogging his dun-pony forward again, his back towards me as I stepped clear of my cover, my gun-hand full of nothingness. 'Don't turn around, Crevis. Just stop your horse and raise your hands high!'

The surprise jerked him upright in the saddle. For a second it seemed he was going to turn and blow my ruse sky-high, but then, cursing, he halted his pony with a jerk of his reins and raised his arms. I moved in behind him, reached up and slipped the .44 from his holster. It had been surprisingly easy. 'Now dismount!'

He cursed again, but swung from his saddle. Once on the ground, he turned to see who had waylaid him.

'Jim Bannerman!' His lips twisted into a sneer, but the sneer disappeared as he saw he was covered by his own pistol. 'Hey, you didn't have no gun!'

'Where's them cattle?' I demanded.

'What cattle?' he responded.

'Crevis, you damned well know . . . '
I trailed off, realizing that I was wasting
my time. I was already certain the
Herefords were up ahead of me, and
precious minutes were slipping by. I
was armed now, and I had a mount;
it was time I made tracks. But as
I turned towards the pony, another
question loomed in my mind.

'What's there between your brother
and Janet Shaughnessy?'

His grin was suddenly working
overtime. 'Why, nothing,' he said,
' 'cepting plans for a wedding.'

'You're a damned liar!' My finger
tightened on the trigger. He knew
how close he was to death because
the colour drained from his face. I
grabbed his shirt, rammed the .44
into his belly and jerked him close to
me. 'Tell me, Crevis, tell me you're a
doggone liar!'

But before he could answer, a horse
whinnied from along the trail behind us.
Foolishly, I half turned. Crevis lunged

away from me, his mouth opening to unleash a warning, but I smashed the barrel of the gun across his head. The cry died in his throat. He dropped like a stone. Leaping over him, I grabbed desperately for the reins of the suddenly bucking dun-pony.

When Sam Crevis and his sheep-herding cattle-rustlers rounded the bend, I was mounted up and in the centre of the trail. Heel-thumping my new-found mount into motion, I blasted them a welcome with the .44, and this had them scattering — and there in their midst was Sam Crevis, clutching his side and then toppling off his animal.

I grunted with satisfaction, at the same time jerking the dun-pony off the trail and up the slope. A bullet cleaved the air close by me, panicking my mount into greater effort. I blazed off two shots over my shoulder. Branches clawed at me and left red weals along the flanks of the pony, but soon we had burst clear of the timber and were topping a hog-backed ridge. Before dipping into the ravine beyond, I glanced back. They were spread across the trail, some mounted, some now on foot. Several were grouped around the fallen Crevises. Then I heard the grunt of horses following up through the trees, and knew I was being pursued. As I reached the bottom of the ravine, two riders crossed the ridge.

I halted the pony, swung about and drew a bead on the first of my pursuers. The shot went low, but it had his horse rearing up, throwing him off. I fired at the second rider but missed. His replying shot jerked yards wide of me by his lunging mount.

Thrusting the pistol into my belt, I pointed the dun-pony down the ravine and slapped him into his fastest gallop. He was game and wiry, with a fair turn of speed, and soon my sheepherding friends were left far behind.

After an hour's southward gallop through twisting ravines I reckoned I was safe from pursuit and I relaxed.

In the afternoon I linked up with the

trail again, and now the mountains were towering close at hand. During my ride I'd done a fair amount of surmising. My clash with the sheepherders had proved that Frank hadn't put in an appearance. Still, by this time he couldn't be far behind me — unless he too was fighting it out with the sheepherders. It now seemed obvious the sheepherders must have got the rustled stock across the river before the rains came. Had poor Ben Wells not survived long enough to spread the news, it might have been several days before the Double Horseshoe became aware of what had happened. Then a new thought occurred to me. I winced at its implications. If anything had happened to Carlos, Frank might still not be any the wiser.

As I pushed on through the afternoon's heat, fresh droppings and hoof-marks told me I was closing on the herd fast. I frequently glanced back, hoping to see signs of support, but behind me the trail was quiet.

It wasn't hard to figure who was ahead of me. Unscrupulous Mexicans had often ridden north, purchased stolen cattle at cut price from rustlers and then whisked them back across the border into obscurity.

In the saddle-boot nestled Tom Crevis's Sharps repeater, and it was on this that my slender hopes of thwarting the Mexicans depended. My appetite had been appeased by the jerked mutton I'd found in one of the saddle bags. Altogether, Tom had proved himself an obliging fellow; though I guessed next time he rode point he'd be more alert.

It was early evening when I heard the bellowing of cattle ahead of me and from then on I kept to the high, pine-cloaked mountain slopes flanking the trail. Dusk was creeping in as I glimpsed the herd and heard the high, excitable cries of Mexicans.

I paced the herd until it was dark, keeping hidden in the trees, and after a while the noise died out below me, which meant the cattle had been allowed to rest. Soon the glimmer of small cooking-fires showed in the darkness. The Mexicans were making camp for the night.

I tethered the pony high up the slope amid the pines, and rested for a couple of hours. It was tonight or never if I was to play my hand, for the border was now a mere morning's ride away. I wished Frank would suddenly come pounding down the trail, backed by a swarm of Double Horseshoe riders — but he didn't.

With night well under way, I drew the Sharps repeater, stuffed my pockets with ammunition from the saddle-bags, and crept down through the trees.

9

At the bottom of the slope, I crouched back in the rocks and took stock. Directly opposite was a canyon, comparatively small and apparently boxed in at the far end. It was into this canyon that the herd had been driven. The Mexicans had pitched camp along its wall. Their blanket-huddled forms were visible against the two campfires. A deathly hush hung over the place. From the trail you'd never have suspected that two-hundred head of run-off stock were concealed so near by.

I worked my way back along the trail for a hundred yards, keeping in the shadows, then I made the crossing at a fast run, dropping down amid boulders on the other side. I paused, senses alert, wondering if any sentries posted near the canyon mouth had spotted me, but the only sound I heard was the uneven rasp of my own breathing.

Gripping the Sharps, I edged forward, climbing all the while. I came to a sheer rock face and skirted it and found myself in a narrow, steeply-angled draw. As I contemplated my next move, my foot dislodged a stone and I cursed as it went down, but after a moment of anxious listening I started to climb again.

It took me a half-hour to reach the back end of that canyon. It was boxed all right, and the ground dipped away sharply where I was. There was no option but to descend that forbidding wall, and hunkering down in the bushes I tried to calculate the best line of action.

At its greatest width the canyon was about seventy yards, with cattle spread right across it. The herd stirred restfully as it settled for the night. I could see the black shadows of three riders, one on each flank of the herd and the other near the canyon mouth.

A slight movement in the inky shadows of a cut-back in the rock down on my right had me puzzled, then I heard the blowing of a horse. I got me an idea. The remuda was down in that cut-back. If I could get down there . . .

Easing clear of the cover, I lowered myself over the lip of the ridge. The moon was bright, and for sixty agonizing seconds I clambered down that precipitous slope in full view had anybody cared to look up, but still there came no sign of alarm from below. After that, the gradient became less steep, and I had ample cover.

I took a breather on reaching the canyon's floor, then I belly-snaked through the rocks towards the remuda. I could hear the horses pulling at the short grass. Then I glimpsed the glimmer of the wrangler's cigarette.

He was sitting on a rock, a rifle slanted across his knees, while behind him some fifteen animals were tethered to a pegged-down guy-rope.

Glancing across to the main encampment, I saw that the Mexicans' fires had died down, and the sound of men's snores carried to me on the still night air.

My attention returned to the wrangler and I inched forward, holding my gun off the ground; the slightest clink would have me discovered. I strained every muscle in my body to subdue the slightest suggestion of a sound. Sweat was running down my face. The herd in the canyon had ceased all stirring and become peaceful, leaving a hush that would grab greedily at any noise I might make.

I was twenty feet clear of them, when the horses ceased chewing. I froze as the wrangler stood up. The cigarette out of his mouth, his head cocked on one side, listening. It seemed a whole age he stayed like that, but at last he placed the smoke back between his lips and sat down again. He must have been satisfied that all was well because he began to sing softly to himself.

The horses weren't so easily put at rest however. They knew something was afoot and were really spooked as I crawled around them. The Mexican's singing ceased; he rose once more, cursing the animals to be still.

I came out of the shadows at the back of him. He turned just too late as he heard the swish of the rifle-butt through the air. The solid thud of steel-bound wood meeting bone had the horses rearing and whinnying in terror. The wrangler was sprawled face down on the ground, and at his hip was a sheathed knife. I pulled the knife clear. The horses were fighting against their ropes, frantic for freedom. I severed the guy-rope with a single slash, then, resting the rifle-butt against my thigh blasted two shots skywards, at the same time yelling at the top of my voice. The horses were away, bursting into the main canyon as if pursued by Satan.

Seconds later the air was filled with alarmed bellows from the cattle and wild Mexican shouting. Returning to the rocks, I unleashed three shots in the direction of the rising din. 'Stampede, you devils! Stampede!' I screamed with all the power of my lungs.

A Mexican was riding towards me, moving between the canyon wall and the wheeling cattle. I took aim and fired and he spun from his saddle, arms thrown high.

The swirling dust was thickening; the ground was shaking with the pound of eight-hundred hooves, and the shouts of the Mexicans lifted shrilly above the bedlam. Crazed with fear, the cattle were fighting and colliding in the attempt to win clear of the canyon.

Through the dust, I glimpsed the men around the fire-glimmer leaping from their blankets and, ramming more shells into the breech, I fired a volley among them, scattering them. Then the weaving mass of the herd enveloped them, their cries drowned by thundering hooves.

I lay in the rocks at the back-end,

gasping for breath. The pandemonium was deafening, the very walls of the canyon reverberating; I'd started something that no man could stop. The herd was stampeding from the canyon.

In the final moments, a dozen or so steers, finding their exit blocked, swung back towards me. They pounded through the dust, the sweep of their great horns showing white. I leaped up, desperately seeking to escape; I ran towards the slope but stumbled over a rock and fell. It seemed the ground was jumping beneath me as I sprawled helpless, awaiting the sickening smash of hooves.

Those Herefords passed so close I smelt the reek of their hair and manure and felt the scorch of the breath on my body, but by nothing less than a miracle neither hoof nor horn took advantage of my vulnerable frame.

Seconds later, incredulously raising my eyes, I watched the bobbing twist of their hindquarters as they followed the wall of the canyon round and finally swung back towards the now open way into the main valley.

I sat up; the bedlam had given way to the fading rumble of the cattle. My trembling legs refused to support my weight as I tried to stand, and I collapsed. How those Herefords had missed me I would never know.

I made it at the second attempt; I watched the dust settle in the empty canyon. But it wasn't quite empty. I could see the unmoving humps. I couldn't tell whether they were trampled-down steers or Mexican thieves.

The thunder of hooves had faded now, the herd scattered into the mountains, but this didn't worry me. The round-up was something I couldn't attempt alone, but the beasts wouldn't stray so far as to be irrecoverable.

I salvaged a blanket and shook the dirt from it, found a canteen of water and drank. After that, I walked from the canyon, crossed the trail, and presently found the dun-pony waiting in the pines where I'd left him.

I watered him the best I could, thankful to have at least one ally. Afterwards, I wrapped myself in the blanket and sprawled down on the soft pine-needles, allowing the sleep of utter weariness to close over me.

The morning was bright when I awoke, the woods alive with wild creatures, and the air rich with the scent of the pines. Through the branches the sky showed a rich blue. For a while I listened to the saucy chatter of the birds, then the dun-pony swung his head and eyed me, wondering what the day held in store for him.

From the position of the sun, I guessed the time was about eleven. I'd had a good sleep and felt refreshed. Having breakfasted on the remaining jerked mutton, I saddled the pony. Frank's assistance was now imperative.

Soon I was edging down through the pines and as I came onto the more sparsely timbered section of the slope,

I could see the sun-shadowed gash of the canyon's opening. It all looked so peaceful now; it seemed impossible that such chaos had occurred there last night. For a second I found myself wondering if it hadn't all been a fantastic nightmare; then I spotted three buzzards circling and all doubt left my mind. I nudged the dun-pony into a canter, anxious to leave the place.

I recalled Tom Crevis's words when I'd asked him what was between his brother and Janet Shaughnessy . . . *Why nothing, 'cepting a few plans for a wedding!*

I'd gunned Sam down, maybe put him out of the reckoning for good, but there was small satisfaction from that. If Janet had agreed to a marriage, then I'd . . . Oh hell, what good was there fretting over what might be?

And yet, I kept recalling the firm clasp of her hand that day in Coltville, and the warmth of her eyes as they'd met mine, and inside me was the heart-hammering feeling that she wanted me

129

as badly as I did her.

At midday, I shot a prairie-hen and kindled a fire to cook it. An hour later, sitting sucking the bones, I heard horses approaching. I stood up, hastily stamping out the embers of the fire, then, cradling my gun, I led the dun-pony back into the trees. As the first rider appeared, I had my sights flush on him. I could easily have killed Wint Craig right then. Backing him came Frank, white-haired Jess Fulcher and six Double Horseshoe men. I lowered my gun and called to them.

As they pulled in about me, Frank was saying, 'Where in all hell have you been?' Then, before I could answer: 'What's happened to them cattle, Jim?'

I waved my arm airily. 'They're scattered in the mountains, just a-waiting to be rounded up. I stampeded them last night — caused one heck of a mess-up.' I paused, savouring his amazement, then went on. 'But it's taken you a mighty long time to arrive. What kept you?'

Frank frowned. 'Bridge was down. We had to ride clear to Barnwell before we could cross the river!'

'Seen any sheepherders along the trail?' I asked.

He shook his head. 'You're the first sign of life since Barnwell.' Then he was suddenly smiling and he gave me a hearty thump on the back. 'Jim, you done damned well. I guess you ain't such a bad kid brother after all!'

I might have been smiling as well, but I wasn't because my glance swung to Wint Craig's mean face; his scowl froze every vestige of well-being from me.

★ ★ ★

It took us a week to round up those cattle. If it hadn't been for the brooding feeling that Pa should have been alongside me, it would've seemed like the old days. Frank and I rode stirrup to stirrup. We were real close to each other for that period, and

I almost came to think we were getting to understand each other again.

There were ten of us, and we got through the work of twice that number. As the stock was driven in from the mountains, we herded them into a small canyon.

Wint Craig toiled as hard as any of us. Sometimes I would turn and find him staring at me, but no words passed between us. I wondered what his real intentions were. As far as the men were concerned, a couple had known him before, and the others, knowing his type, were afraid of him and so treated him with extreme courtesy.

Frank and I didn't discuss our problems, but put all our efforts into our work. My brother was undoubtedly the boss among the men, at times I could see Pa in him, and I admired him for the way he got things moving.

These were days of hard riding and nights of sleeping with the stars fresh and clear above our heads. Hard work and clean air put a keen edge on my appetite, and at night I slept dreamlessly, awaking refreshed.

On the fifth day I saw Wint Craig shake hands with Frank and ride off.

Reading the unspoken question in my eyes, Frank told me, 'He's going into Coltville to meet some of his bunkies. They're gonna help us out.' Before I had time to raise the old arguments, he turned and walked away.

Later that morning Frank and I rode to the west through steep ravines. There was plenty of cattle-sign beckoning us on, and presently Frank called and pointed towards the far end of the valley we'd just entered. Against the green background of pines, I glimpsed six grass-fat steers.

'Reckon we can make this the last batch,' Frank announced. 'We'll grab them, then cut our losses.'

We crossed the valley in a wide loop. The steers lifted their heads enquiringly, then lit out stubbornly. But soon we'd hazed them into a gulley, and after that we had them buttoned up as neat as

Aunt Meg's sewing.

Once sure of our quarry, we took a breather. Frank led his sorrel down the gulley to a stream. Intending to follow suit in a moment, I sat down on a small boulder and fumbled with rice-paper shuck and tobacco. I lit up, enjoying the richness of the smoke, then leaned back a little. Behind me was the sheer face of the cliff, reaching up, high and green-topped, towards the sky. I took another draw on my cigarette and my gaze happened to swing across to the dun-pony, some twelve feet away . . .

That glance saved my life! The animal's eyes were rolled upward in sudden alarm. He unleashed a terrified whinny, rearing back. In that instant came a great swoosh in the air. Blind instinct had me hurling myself to the side. There was a mighty, ground-shaking thud and splintering crack of rock against rock — then silence.

A huge boulder had crashed down onto the very spot where I'd been sitting a split second before.

Frank came rushing up, his face white. Together we looked towards the cliff-edge, a hundred feet above. The only movement came from a big buzzard, wing-flapping its way clear of a ledge near the top.

'Might've been a natural fall,' Frank said.

We circled round and ten minutes later emerged onto the cliff top. It was easy to see where the great boulder had been precariously poised. The hard ground was bare of tracks and we searched about for quite a time without finding the slightest sign that it had been anything but an accident — a fluke of nature.

★ ★ ★

When we started the herd homeward, we were only twenty short of the number originally stolen. Yet it rankled to think that the sheepherders had made their cash, and, apart from the Crevis brothers, had got away unscathed.

The river by now had returned to its normal level, and we crossed the herd between the lakes. We drove the cattle hard after that, not letting them rest until we were close to the Double Horseshoe. When we finally rode into the ranch all was in darkness, apart from lights burning in the Vasquez cabin, and as we dismounted in the yard, Carlos hurried out to hear the news.

'And good things have happened here as well,' said the Mexican, grinning proudly. 'It's a boy!' And from his cabin came the lusty yells of a fresh-born babe.

Mattie appeared in the doorway looking harassed, her hair awry, but she gave an excited shout and came running to meet us, her eyes filled with tears of happy relief.

10

He turned a cold eye to my cheerful greeting. I tried the apologetic approach, but was ignored. Finally, I gave him a dig in the ribs. Only then did he swing his head, nudge my hand and nicker that all was forgiven.

'You old devil, Copper!' I exclaimed. 'How in tarnation did you get yourself out of that river?'

Carlos paused in the currying of the dun-pony. 'Meester Jim, when Copper came back without you, none of us dared speak what we feared in our hearts.'

Yes, the gallant chestnut had pulled through. Only he knew how he'd escaped the wrath of the storm-lashed river, and he wasn't telling. He was in good shape.

Carlos and I left the barn, and I went to his cabin to see the new papoose.

Maria was radiant, and the baby boy, gurgling happily, looked every bit as sturdy as her other children. He had Carlos's twinkle in his eye.

'What's his name, Maria?' I asked.

'Carlos says it is to be James,' she smiled.

'It is a fine name,' Carlos murmured. 'The boy will have something to live up to, Meester Jim.'

I laughed. Inwardly I was telling myself that peace must be restored in Grand Valley, if only to ensure James Vasquez would have a safe place to grow up in.

* * *

Next morning Mattie and I went for a ride. Circling the herd, we exchanged nods with Ed Hunter and old-timer Jess Fulcher who were keeping watch, guns ever alert. Mattie had been full of questions about my experiences with the rustlers, and it wasn't until we were making tracks for home that I recalled

Gregg Miller's earnest request.

'Gregg saved my life in town the other day,' I said.

'Gregg . . . ?' She stiffened at mention of his name.

'Sure. Stepped right in when my goose was nigh cooked. Lucky for me he can handle a gun.' I drew Copper close to her horse. 'He's mighty fond of you, Mattie. Why don't you let him see you?'

We reined in our horses on a hillock, the great rolling prairie stretching away in front of us. She tried an abrupt switch of subject. 'This sure is lovely country, Jim. Just look how clear those mountains show up today.' But there was a catch in her voice, and I knew she wasn't thinking about the scenery, or the clearness of the day.

'Why don't you give him a chance to tell you how much he loves you?' I persisted. 'He's worth it.'

She looked down. 'Poor Gregg,' she whispered. 'I told him that if the law didn't do something . . . '

'He's doing everything in his power. Maybe he could do a lot more if you were alongside to help out.'

For a while she sat in silence. Eventually she said, 'I'll see him soon, but not yet — not just yet.' And she spurred her mount forward over the rise.

We returned to the ranch and dismounted. Frank appeared. With him were four strangers and Wint Craig. The newcomers reminded me of the buzzards I'd seen in the stampede-canyon. After a brief conversation which included introductions, Craig led his bunkies off in the direction of the bunk-house.

I noticed Frank's satisfied smile. I followed him into the house. He sat down and filled a couple of glasses with whiskey. I sank into a chair and we drank.

'When are you planning to make your move?' I asked.

'Tomorrow night. You know, we ain't as strong as I'd hoped for. Wint

140

expected at least ten of his boys to show up, but so far there's only four. He reckons it may be a week or so before the rest roll in. But I'm damned sure we can smash them sheepherders with what we've got.' He refilled his glass. 'You riding with us, Jim?'

I hesitated, then said, 'I guess so, Frank.' Then I thought of Janet, and I was torn between family loyalty and the awful prospect of seeing her hurt.

When it was time for me to take my turn riding herd that afternoon, I rested Copper and rode my sorrel.

While watching the cattle, I was haunted by the thought of the bloody havoc Wint Craig's killers could cause. Plenty of sheepherders deserved the worst, but there were also innocent women and kids; Frank's hatred was such that he would make no effort to restrain Craig.

By the time Ed Hunter and the relief shift were riding out to take over, I'd reached a decision. A search of Pa's death-place had thrown no light on the identity of his killer, nor had a meeting with that no-good marshal. It seemed that I had one more alternative. I had just twenty-four hours in which to find out how much old John Shaughnessy was blinded by bitterness.

Ed Hunter nodded to me as he rode up, unsheathing his rifle and thumbing shells into its breech. 'The bastards ain't catching us asleep again,' he remarked.

'All been peaceful so far,' I told him. 'Look, when you get back, tell Frank I've gone to see John Shaughnessy, but I won't be giving away any secrets.'

Hunter swung round. 'Why, man, you're plumb loco!' I didn't linger. I spurred the sorrel towards the river.

★ ★ ★

Much of the heat had left the day as I forded the Ute and rode up past those sun-bleached sheep bones. There wasn't a whisper of breeze; even the birds seemed silent.

Brack and Nat Shaughnessy were burned up with hatred for the Bannermans; why should I suppose their father was different? Still, it was too late now for misgivings. I wondered where Emma, Janet's mother, figured in all this. I knew she would never have advocated violence, for she was a gentle woman. It was not from her that Brack and Nat had inherited their viciousness.

I was determined not to betray Frank. He was playing things by the only rules he knew. But although I wanted Pa's killer brought to justice and the valley shed of sheepherders, I didn't want to see the innocent gunned down, and I couldn't live with the thought of Janet being in danger. Yet all my reasoning was to no avail; I was bushwhacked a mile beyond the river.

I'd been going cautiously, with the Sharps ready across my saddle, but near the lower mouth of the arroyo in which the Mulheron cabin was situated, I was forced to ride close to the trees. They must have been waiting for me. Too late I glimpsed the poised figure of a man, his gun raised as he drew a bead on me.

The shot blasted the silence open, and a searing pain hammered into my shoulder, jerking me backwards out of the saddle. I didn't have much recollection of hitting the ground; all I remember was seeing my rifle twisting from my grasp, flying away through the air . . .

I tried to shake the muzziness from my head. My shirt was soggy with blood. I was dimly aware of the sorrel high-tailing away up the arroyo.

A toe was hooked under my belly and I was jerked over. I yelled with the pain in my shoulder; a figure looming over me gradually came into focus — Sam Crevis! Behind him I could see Nat Shaughnessy reloading his gun.

With purposeful fingers, Crevis unbuttoned his shirt, drew it open and revealed his chest. He turned slightly to show a red groove across his lower ribs.

'See that, Bannerman?' he snarled. Grabbing my shirt-front he wrenched me up. I was wincing with agony, and I could feel blood streaming down my side. 'You did that — and by Christ, you're gonna suffer for it!'

Everything around me spun dizzily as Nat Shaughnessy got his hands beneath my arm-pits and jerked me onto my feet. I just stood there, swaying, until the sharp sting of a face-slap snapped my head up and brought me temporarily to my senses. When I attempted to move my arms I realized they'd lashed my wrists together.

'Just give me a chance to talk with old man Shaughnessy.' I was sick at having to plead with them.

Crevis smashed the back of his hand across my face, his flashy ring cutting my cheek. 'Like hell!' he spat.

I collapsed. Red mists merged into blackness.

★ ★ ★

Consciousness returned, bringing with it agonizing pain. I could see the flickering movement of light which gradually took the shape of a blazing fire about ten yards distant. Around it lazed several men, their voices murmuring. We were in a clearing of the wood. My feet were dangling off the ground. I was hanging by my wrists which were lashed to a branch. My shirt had been ripped from my back and it seemed there was blood all over me.

I realized that the men grouped around the fire had stopped talking. My nostrils widened to the reek of whiskey, and looking down I saw Brack Shaughnessy holding an uncorked bottle. The fire was glinting on his teeth.

'Waal,' he drawled, 'boys, our guest has just woken up. You ain't been much company up to now, Bannerman. Have a drop of this. It'll make you more sociable!'

They began to laugh — Sam Crevis,

Nat Shaughnessy, Mich Edwards, Paddy Mulheron and a couple more I'd never seen before — and every one hankering to see me dead!

The bottle was rammed between my lips and tilted. Liquid fire hit my throat. I spluttered and coughed.

Brack stood back, corking the bottle. 'That's perked you up. Can't have you pegging out — not yet.'

Sam Crevis brushed Brack aside and stood looking up at me. 'You ain't gonna die so easy as your ole man did,' he snarled. He began to roll up his sleeves. 'Fancy a punk like you thinking hisself man enough to marry Janet. Thank God she's come to her senses!'

He turned and walked over to where their horses were tethered. He unstrapped something from his saddle.

The fire was leaping high, setting crazy shadows dancing. It was like a nightmare — but the agony in my shoulder assured me it was no dream. My tormentors were staring at me with expressions of smouldering hatred.

Sam Crevis stepped back into the circle of light. He was uncoiling a bull-whip.

Slowly, he walked around me. They were all on their feet, cigarettes trampled into the dirt. They wanted me dead all right — but first they wanted to see me squirm!

I heard the hiss of Crevis's indrawn breath, and then the wicked sing of thong biting through air. I tensed myself for the lash, but Crevis flicked it aside. The others laughed; this was the sort of sport they enjoyed. Their faces hardened again. I could feel sweat stinging the wound in my shoulder. Everything in the clearing was tinged with hazy redness.

When the lash came, Crevis's voice was shrieking with each stroke . . . *'This is for what you done to Janet . . . This is for running me down . . . This is for putting a bullet in my ribs . . .'*

A million blood-red lights were exploding in my head, and with them a million agonies!

11

There was no pain now, only the feeling that I was drifting beyond suffering. Once, far-off voices probed into the mists of my awareness; but they were replaced by a voice which was soothing. With it came the touch of gentle hands, bringing a coolness to my forehead. The mists merged into full darkness; the glimmerings of consciousness gave way to sleep.

The voice came again. For all I could tell an hour, a day, a week might have passed since last I'd heard it. Still, I could find no real light, only those vague swirling mists through which my only guidance was the calmness of the voice and the firm yet soft touch . . .

★ ★ ★

Water was being poured into a bowl. I could hear the heavy breathing of somebody. After a while I could see a ceiling that was ornamented and had lamp shadows playing across it. I could smell oil burning. My eyes closed tight, then opened again, and things drifted into place.

I was in a room, lying on a bed with a blanket covering me. Nearby I could see the broad back of a man who had finished washing and was drying his hands on a towel. At last he turned, and the heavy-jowled features and kindly grey eyes were familiar. I moved my lips, surprised to find my voice no more than a husky whisper.

'You're Doc Wilmer . . . '

He came quickly towards me and his hand touched my shoulder. His touch was gentle, but not the same . . . 'Rest, man, rest. You've come a long way.'

And I closed my eyes and slept.

I awoke much later. He was sitting in a rocking-chair across the room. Sunlight was streaming through an open window. He had been watching me; now he stood up and came over to my bed. I tried to sit up, but winced as sharp pain stabbed my shoulder. I fell back.

'Easy, man.' He checked the bandage around my shoulder.

It all came back to me: the whip-lash, Sam Crevis's harsh voice, the fire blazing before my swimming eyes.

'How did I get here?' I asked.

'You were brought to me,' he said. 'You'd have died otherwise. It took me an hour to dig that bullet out of your shoulder. It was a blessing you weren't conscious.'

'But who . . . ?' Then I recalled the gentle voice and hands. After a moment I said, 'Janet Shaughnessy.'

He nodded. 'They left you for dead. She heard them laughing and boasting about it. After searching around for hours, she found you, still strung up to a tree.'

I felt a surge of excitement. 'Where is she now?'

'She's been here for two days, sitting by you. When we knew for sure that you'd pull through, she left. She said it would be better for you not to see her.'

'But . . . ' This time I made it into a sitting position, but the words died behind my gritted teeth as pain swept over me. 'When — when did she leave?'

'Four hours ago,' he said. 'Now, get some sleep.'

* * *

That evening Gregg Miller came to visit me. He gave a wide smile. 'My God, Jim, you took some pummelling.'

I gripped his coat sleeve. 'What's been going on?'

He frowned. 'Your brother, Wint Craig and the rest of 'em attacked the sheepherders the night afore last. Burned a couple of cabins, including the Mulherons'. But the sheepherders were stronger than they'd counted on, and there was a big fight in the Mulheron ravine. One of your Double Horseshoe men was killed and several wounded, but I don't know about the sheepherders.' He wiped his lips with the back of his hand. 'Wint Craig came into Coltville this morning to see Dainton. I could hear them talking through the door. He said Crevis and his crowd crossed the river last night and tried to run off some cattle, but there was another fight and they were turned back before they could strike. Dammit, Jim, things are getting out of hand. I spent all afternoon trying to talk sense into Dainton's skull — but it was hopeless.'

It was plain that Gregg was on the verge of a show-down with Dainton. I didn't prompt him, but waited in silence for his mind to wrestle out its own conclusions.

Eventually he got to his feet. 'Jim,' he said, 'I'll give Dainton another week. If he's done nothing by then,

I'm riding to Dalton to get the county sheriff.'

Not much later Doc Wilmer came in, saying it was time for me to rest. Gregg said, 'See you soon, Jim.'

After he'd gone Wilmer turned the lamp down. 'Doc,' I said, 'how long am I gonna be hog-tied to this bed?'

He shrugged his shoulders. 'Maybe four days — maybe ten. Depends on how those lashes heal and your shoulder mends. Count yourself lucky to be alive. You must have the constitution of a grizzly!'

That night sleep didn't come easy. I was recovered enough to do some serious thinking. Janet had saved my life. The knowledge of this had me restless to be on my feet and searching for her. What else could her actions mean other than that she still loved me? And yet why had she walked out when I was nearing consciousness? I was haunted by Sam Crevis's words: *You ain't gonna die so easy as your old man did* . . . and about Janet:

Thank God that gal's finally come to her senses.

Was he bluffing? By the way he'd spoken, he'd killed Pa himself — and was marrying Janet next week!

It was as well that I hadn't got the strength to get up, otherwise I'd have gone gunning for him right then.

Frank, Mattie and Carlos came next morning. Somehow they'd found out what had happened. I expected Frank to rave on about my stupidity. I think that would have been easier to bear than his attitude of reproachful silence.

Mattie did most of the talking during the visit, while Carlos, looking worried, kept near the window so he could see who was in the street, and note what interest the sight of a Bannerman wagon in town aroused.

★ ★ ★

Mattie's main concern was with my hurts, but after I had convinced her that I was nowhere near dying, she

155

told me about the sheepherders' second attempt to run off the cattle. It seemed she had witnessed the fight from up on the knoll close to the ranch. The attack came as revenge for Frank's burning of the Mulheron homestead, but it had misfired from the start because Ed Hunter, spotting them crossing the river, had raised the alarm.

'Sure was terrible, even so,' Mattie concluded.

'I don't like you being here, Jim,' Frank grunted. 'If they found out, they'd rip this house apart.'

'Doc Wilmer reckons about four days and I'll be fit for travelling,' I said, and I was suddenly wondering how Janet had explained things to her folks — and to Crevis.

'Yeah,' said Frank, far from satisfied, 'well, we'll be in and get you home just as soon as Doc says okay.'

When they'd departed I felt mighty vulnerable. If Crevis was to walk through the door, I'd be helpless. I got Doc to fetch me a six-shooter from the town's gunsmith's, and from then on I kept it within easy reach.

During the week, Gregg visited me often, and as the days passed my wounds healed well and my strength returned. On Sunday I was allowed up for the first time. The church bell was tolling its invitation to worship, and soon hymns came slow and melodious. It sounded so peaceful and good; it seemed unbelievable that just a few miles away men were plotting to kill each other.

Frank was coming that morning to take me home. Gregg had told me that he'd finally quit with Dainton. He intended riding out that evening for Dalton to let Joe Shayman, the county sheriff, know what was going on.

My brother, Carlos and Mattie arrived on the stroke of eleven. They came in a wagon. I was shaky on my legs as I expressed my thanks to Doc Wilmer. I paid him his fee, which he'd earned ten times over, then Frank and I stepped outside. Carlos was standing in an adjacent doorway, keeping watch. Mattie was talking to Gregg on the sidewalk; it was good to see them together again.

Doc Wilmer helped me into the wagon, and when I was settled he said, 'I've worked hard patching you up, Jim Bannerman. You go and get yourself killed after all my efforts, and I'll never raise my hand to help you again!'

I laughed. 'I'll take care — and thanks again.'

Gregg and Mattie came across to the wagon, their arms linked. If ever a man had woman-love in his eyes, then Gregg had it right now. The way Mattie looked, any man would've been proud to have her on his arm.

But almost immediately the ever-present threat of violence destroyed the serenity of that Sunday morning. Carlos came running over. 'Riders just pulled into the other end of the street! They're not our boys!'

'Let's go,' Frank said, climbing on to the wagon.

Gregg and Mattie exchanged worried glances. Mattie stepped towards the wagon, aware of the need to move out, but suddenly she swung back and slipped her arms around Gregg's neck. They kissed, then he helped her into the wagon, and Frank whipped the horse into motion.

I glanced back at Gregg waving farewell to us, at the same time wondering when we would see him again. Marshal Dainton had spoken threateningly of *the displeasure of certain elements in Coltville* if law was brought in from Dalton — what the hell had he meant?

As we raced out of the street and into the open country, I felt sure that Gregg Miller was letting himself in for plenty of trouble. The happiness shining in Mattie's eyes doubled my apprehension. The prospect of more sorrows coming her way was a depressing thought.

As we thundered past Hilda Zimm's house, Frank's gaze swung across, but today Hilda didn't show herself. I recalled how she had previously turned back into the house on my approach, as if contact with a Bannerman was to be avoided, and it came to me that things must have gone sadly amiss between her and Frank, but I didn't voice my thoughts. After all, it wasn't my business.

The journey back to the Double Horseshoe was misery. The wagon bumped roughly over the trail as Frank drove the horses, and my wounds protested painfully. The sun's heat had the sting of sweat increasing my discomfort. We kept a constant watch on our back-trail, but saw nothing to indicate pursuit, and finally we arrived back at the Double Horseshoe. By that time I was exhausted, and glad enough for Mattie to help me up to my room for a rest.

There followed a week of frustrating inactivity. Mattie insisted that I was far too weak to fend for myself, and I spent the days sunning myself on the verandah, watching riders move in and out of the ranch.

I learned that the man who had been killed during the clashes of the previous week was Russ Simons, a big, red-headed cowboy from Wyoming. Firstly there'd been Pa, then Ben Wells, Hank Symes and Tom Glint, and now Simons. This was full-scale war by any man's reckoning. The question constantly in my mind was could the intervention of the county sheriff bring peace to Grand Valley? I wondered if Gregg had made it to Dalton. The days dragged on and still there was no news.

If Frank felt badly about the loss of his men, he didn't show it. He bustled about organizing the cattle guards and running the ranch. While he was obsessed with the desire to get rid of the sheepherders, a strange, heavy quietness seemed to hang over the valley. It was, I knew, the lull before the inevitable storm.

Often Maria came across to sit with

me with her new baby, Jim. He was the image of Carlos.

Mattie bathed my back every day, just as Doc Wilmer had done, and by the following Sunday I figured I was pretty much my old self. It was that day that Wint Craig came to the house and spoke long with Frank. I was sitting on the verandah. Craig stepped close to me as he left, and for a second his hard eyes met mine. Then, as Mattie came out, he crossed the yard into the bunk-house.

Mattie perched on the arm of my chair. 'Craig just told Frank he's expecting the rest of his men to get here tomorrow,' she said.

'More or less what I reckoned,' I frowned. I hated the thought of Craig's power increasing; it made me shudder to think how Frank would make use of it. 'Do you think it's right, all this fighting?' I asked Mattie.

She thought for a moment, then replied. 'At first I did, but now I ain't so sure. Gregg was right when

162

he said it'd be best to bring in the county sheriff.'

'You know Gregg left for Dalton the day you collected me from the doc?'

Her brown eyes were full of concern. 'That's what has me worried, Jim. He should've been back afore now.'

'These things sometimes take time,' I consoled her. 'Maybe Shayman had other duties before he could leave. Come to that, maybe they're already in Coltville.'

'I don't think so,' she sighed. 'Oh, if only I could be sure Gregg's not hurt — not . . .'

I suddenly felt angry. My reassurances had convinced her no more than they had me. 'Mattie,' I said firmly, 'I reckon I've been an invalid for too long. I'm riding to Coltville to find out if Gregg's got back.'

'But you ain't fit enough . . .'

I got to my feet. 'We'll see about that!'

12

It was late afternoon and the day's fiercest heat was spent. Copper was striding out as though anxious to make up for his recent lack of exercise, and we made good time along the Coltville trail. After an hour in the saddle my shoulder-wound was playing merry hell. But I was impatient to discover how things stood with Gregg Miller and made no attempt to restrain the willing chestnut.

Hard-learned caution had me glancing over my shoulder often, and once I figured I saw dust lifting far behind me along the trail. I couldn't be certain however, and if it was anybody they certainly weren't interested in me. Nearing Coltville, the land became flat and open and I was the only moving thing in it.

Little would be achieved by barging

hot-neck into trouble again, so I decided to be careful. I skirted the town and tethered Copper in the cottonwoods on the south side. Dusk was setting in as I made my way through the assortment of buildings that flanked the empty and silent main street. There were only three horses hitched outside The Bull Fly. A woman appeared at a doorway, gave me a nervous glance, then hastily went back inside.

A lantern showed through the window of the marshal's office. The outer door was unlocked and, opening it quietly, I stepped inside. From the doorway of the inner office a shaft of light slanted across the floor, and the strong aroma of cigar-smoke pervaded the air. I slipped my gun from its holster, feeling too wound-weak to play heroics, then walked into Dainton's office.

He was adjusting the wick of the lantern, but he straightened up sharply as he heard my step. His cigar nearly dropped from his lips as he stared into the business end of my Colt.

'Why the stick-up, sonny?'

The edge on his voice betrayed his fast-racing mind. Sure as hell, he was calculating his chances of reaching for his own gun. His eyes flicked over my limp-hanging arm, but even so he must have concluded the odds were too great, because he raised his hands.

'I reckoned I might get a few answers out of you this way,' I grunted. 'Tell me where Gregg Miller is!'

'You realize you're holding a gun on a United States marshal,' he said. 'I could pull you in for that.'

'I realize there'll be one punk less in the world if I don't get an answer. Where's Gregg Miller!'

He lowered his hand to remove the cigar from his mouth. 'The last I saw of him was when he rode out for Dalton last week. Like you, he had the damn fool notion of bringing in the law from the county seat.'

'Then why hasn't he done it?' I demanded.

A smug smile was spreading across Dainton's face. 'I told you he was being a fool. Probably he saw sense in what I said and cleared out of Coltville for good.' His eyes were glinting wickedly in the lantern-light.

I switched to another track. 'You told me there were certain elements in Coltville who would be very much against law being brought in from outside. What did you mean by that, Dainton?'

Right then we both heard the thud of hooves in the street outside. I stepped over to the window and peered over the top of the dirty net curtain. Several riders were pulling in outside The Bull Fly. They dismounted and stood talking for a moment, and I cursed because it was too dark to recognize them.

Then one detached himself from the group and stepped up on to the sidewalk and into the saloon and I saw the sharp, unmistakable profile of Mitch Edwards, one of the sheepherders who'd been party to my flogging. If they caught me again, I knew there'd be no second chances.

Dainton saw my uneasiness. 'I wouldn't be lingering if I was in your boots, sonny.'

'I won't linger,' I growled, 'not a second after I've beaten out of you just who would object to some real law in Coltville.' I lowered the gun till it was directed at his protruding belly. 'You'll die real slow with a bullet in your fat guts. Now start talking fast!'

My threat had scared him. 'All right, Bannerman. It's no skin off my nose. But let's be civilized — my arms are aching. Put that gun away. I won't try no tricks.'

I didn't trust him, but I said, 'Okay, but remember my gun hand's not harmed.' I holstered the Colt.

The tension seemed to flow out of him. He lowered his hands, stepped behind his desk and sat down. 'Seems I've got a lot to explain to you, sonny. But first we need a little drink; we're both kinda jumpy.' He found a couple of glasses and slid one across the top of the desk towards me. 'I got whiskey and cigars,' he said. Then he leaned sideways and slid open a drawer — the same drawer in which I'd suspected a gun was hidden on my last visit.

Even I was surprised at the speed of my draw. The Colt was suddenly in my hand, belching flame, filling the room with its blast. Lead ripped into his arm, twisting him backwards out of his chair, on to the floor.

I stepped through the gunsmoke and looked in the drawer. As expected, there was a lethal Derringer pistol lying there — and something else, too. Underneath the gun was a wad of yellow and black hand-bills. I glanced at Dainton. He was sprawled on his belly, whimpering and cursing with the pain of his shattered right arm. Grabbing one of the hand-bills I scanned its bold print.

WANTED
WINSTON CRAIG
DEAD OR ALIVE
REWARD $5,000

Dainton ceased his whimpering. He stared at me with hate-filled eyes. His blood was soaking into the carpet.

'That's your *certain elements*, isn't it?' I rammed the hand-bill into his face. 'Wint Craig!'

A drumming of feet sounded on the planking outside. I didn't wait to see who the visitor was. There was an open window at the back end of the office. I clambered through it, landing on all fours in the dirt outside. Scrambling to my feet, I ran into the darkness. I could hear voices shouting behind me.

I ran, twisting through the dark hulks of sheds and barns, forcing my weakened frame to even greater efforts as pursuing footsteps sounded from behind.

The open doorway of a barn loomed before me. I blundered through it, stumbling amid the straw inside.

Gulping for breath, I heard feet go rushing past. A voice yelled out, 'Where the hell did he go?' And then to my utter relief some misguided fool answered, 'Must've doubled back that way!' After a moment, I heard them scrambling off on a false trail, and soon all was silent.

My main fear now was that they might find Copper in the trees where I'd left him tethered.

Soaked in sweat, I lay in the straw, waiting for my limbs to stop shaking. From behind me came the movements of an animal, indignant at having company. I eased further back into the blackness, and it was then I realized the hand-bill was still in my clenched fist.

Why hadn't Dainton blazed Wint Craig's wanted-notice across town? He was clearly trying to shield the outlaw. It was Craig who wanted no outside lawmen in Coltville.

Remembering the original aim of my

trip, I clambered up. Maybe right now Gregg Miller was sprawled somewhere along the Dalton trail with a bullet in his back!

I was about to quit the barn when I heard approaching footsteps. I froze in the shadows. Two men moved into the dim light of the opening and paused there, panting from exertion. One of them was Mitch Edwards. He turned to his companion and grunted, 'I guess that doggone eel has given us the slip again. I swear he won't do it no third time, though.'

The other man spat into the dust. 'Anyway, where's this house, Mitch?' he asked.

'Yeah . . . Round up the boys. We'll hit the Bannermans in a way they ain't reckoned for. It's that big white house outside of town. Frank Bannerman's woman lives there — alone. It'll burn like tinder, I guess.'

They were gone then, leaving me with a vision of a slim, graceful figure with corn-yellow hair — Hilda Zimm.

My God, they were going to set fire to her house!

I crept from the barn, and keeping to the shadows ran towards the trees above the town. Once, I saw men moving down towards the main street — but I made sure they didn't see me. For ten minutes I kept to the timber, then having satisfied myself that nobody else was around, I cut down the slope onto the out-of-town trail.

Soon I was opening the gate of Hilda Zimm's house. I stepped on to the verandah and hammered on the oak door.

It was no longer of any consequence how Hilda felt towards the Bannermans; she was in big trouble because of us and for that reason I had to help her.

I glanced to my left, and though the trail from town was currently empty, I figured it wasn't going to remain so for long. Again I hammered on the door. At last sounds came from inside and then bolts were drawn back. The door swung open just a few inches and the whiteness of a face showed in the glow of a lantern.

'Who's there?' Hilda Zimm enquired, but before I could answer she recognized me and spoke my name.

'Listen, Hilda,' I gasped. 'Sheepherders are in town figuring on wrecking your place. They want to get even with Frank. You're in big danger. Let me in!'

She hesitated, but I barged forward and forced the door open. Once inside I slammed it shut and slipped the bolt across, then I turned and grunted with surprise.

I'd always thought Hilda Zimm a beautiful woman, but the sight of her now was breathtaking. Her chemise was transparent, and beneath it her breasts showed clearly.

She placed the lantern down, the light outlining her figure, and as she turned her lips were curved in a smile. 'Well, you're in,' she said. Then she stepped close, her thigh brushing mine.

Her arms slid about my waist, pulling me to her, and the heady fragrance of her perfume enveloped me. There was a wanton desperation in her. For a second I just gazed at her moist lips.

Then her spell was broken by the clumsy thump of somebody moving in the back room.

I pushed her away from me, shaking off her clinging arms. As I blundered up the passage, the angry words that escaped her lips were anything but ladylike! I opened the door and stepped into the main room. It was lit by a huge chandelier, reflecting pin-points of light on the dozens of glass and china ornaments that decorated the place. I crossed the room to where the curtains were billowing inwards in the night breeze. Dragging them back, I realized that I hadn't been the only person to escape through a window that evening! Hooves pounded outside, and suddenly in the moonlight I saw a fast-moving horse and rider show against the trees. In a few moments the sound of hooves faded into the night.

I swung round angrily. She was standing in the doorway, a tumble of yellow hair concealing her face.

'You delayed me just long enough, Hilda,' I grunted.

Her laugh was short, mocking me.

'Who was he, Hilda?'

She threw her hair back with a jerk of her head. 'I ain't saying — and you won't make me. No Bannerman will ever make me do what I don't have a mind to!'

'Anyway,' I said curtly, 'you'd better get some clothes on fast. You're gonna have to come with me.'

Some of the haughtiness faded from her eyes. 'What's happening?' she asked.

I gripped hold of her shoulder. 'Get dressed!'

She gave me an indignant glance and then went.

I found the house's back door and went outside. I looked back along the Coltville trail. Now there was plenty of movement there — a half-dozen flaming torches, bobbing steadily nearer, and carrying clear on the breeze came the thud of heavily rowelled horses.

I ran back inside and yelled at her to hurry. Seconds later she came down the stairs, wrapped in a coat. Her eyes were burning with defiance. I grabbed her arm, but she stiffened and pulled away from me.

'You ain't gonna make me leave this house,' she cried. 'I don't need your help!'

She twisted round and ran into the main room. For a moment I hesitated. I didn't owe this she-cat anything. But then I recalled Ben Wells's pain-twisted features, and the insane lust to kill in the eyes of the sheepherders as they'd whipped me. To them Hilda Zimm was Bannerman-tainted and they'd kill her without hesitation.

I followed after her; she was standing amid her shining ornaments. She was ready to fight, but weakened arm or not I still figured myself a match for any woman. I grabbed her, swung her across my good shoulder and blundered out through the back door. She struggled; it was all I could do to hang on to her; her fists pummelled my back. I covered maybe fifty yards before I was forced to drop her. I dropped to my haunches, still gripping her, and gazed back at the house. What I saw had me flattening both her and myself into the grass.

The fire-raisers had surrounded the house. Soon I could see men through the windows, ransacking the place, and as they came out minutes later, flames were leaping inside the rooms. Riders were driving their horses back and forth, hurling their torches on to the roof. The night became filled with the crackle of flames.

Hilda went crazy; had I not kept her pinned down, she would have run back and tackled them single-handed. Eventually, when sheer exhaustion silenced her ravings, I said, 'My horse is in the trees. Let's go!'

Even then I had doubts. Was it right for me to take her back to the Double Horseshoe? If she'd belonged to Frank once, she certainly didn't now. But there'd be no safety for her elsewhere, so I had no alternative. I shut my mind to the rights and wrongs of it. The main thing was to get clear of Coltville alive!

Copper was waiting where I'd left him. Hilda mounted without help, and swinging up behind her I heeled the chestnut forward, clear of the trees. The house was ablaze, lighting up the surrounding prairie. The fire's hungry roar carried to us, and suddenly Hilda was shuddering and cursing. I realized she was shaking with rage. Any other woman would have been sobbing her eyes out then, but to this one, blaspheming came easier.

★ ★ ★

As we neared the Double Horseshoe, we were challenged by one of Frank's night-guards, but on recognizing my voice we were allowed to pass. It was after midnight when I reined in Copper in the ranch yard. Hilda slipped from the saddle and stood with her head bowed, but she looked up as lights flared in the house. Frank came through the door, rifle in one hand, lantern in the other.

Hilda saw him and called his name. She walked unsteadily towards him. 'They've burned my house,' she snapped, 'and it's all your fault, Frank Bannerman!'

'They'd have killed her if she'd been there,' I said.

But Frank seemed not to hear. He paced forward, his face hateful. 'That house is all you care for,' he cried. 'Just that and those trinkets your ma was crazy over!' He walked down the steps and they stood glaring at each other. 'You ain't got nothing left now,' he said.

'I got you, Frank.' Her voice came bold and sure. 'You know damned well I got you!'

I held my breath. It was dangerous to provoke Frank when he was in this kind of mood, but to my astonishment he took it, nodding in agreement at what she said.

Mattie had appeared, drawing her night-gown about her. 'Jim,' she called, 'did you find out about Gregg?'

Frank seemed oblivious to what was going on about him. I don't think he'd heard Mattie's question. 'Thanks for bringing Hilda in, Jim,' he said. 'You did the right thing.' The hardness had gone out of him as he took hold of Hilda and led her into the house.

'Where's Gregg?' There was panic in Mattie's voice.

I felt exhausted. I nearly toppled from the saddle, but I steadied myself and dismounted. 'I don't know, Mattie,' I said, 'but I aim to find out, even if it means riding clear to Dalton. Just give me a few hours' rest.'

'I'll ride with you, Meester Jim.'

I didn't have to look around to know who was standing behind me in the darkness.

13

Carlos and I circled the sheep country, then forded the river and struck out towards the distant Smoke Mountains. While we rode, I told Carlos about the events of the night before. 'Seems Dainton's dead scared of Craig,' I said. 'He's hushed up the reward posters and done all he can to keep decent law out of the territory. And he's done practically nothing about Pa's murder. I'd like to know if he's shielding Craig in some way over that, too.'

I reined in Copper and swung round to face the Mexican. 'Carlos, I reckon Wint Craig killed my father.'

'But why should he have done that, Meester Jim?'

'Revenge for me shooting him after the bank raid.'

'But why hasn't he tried to kill *you*?'

'I think he has,' I said. 'When we were rounding up the Herefords, I believe he trailed Frank and me — and tried to crush me with that boulder. It missed me, thank God, but I'm sure he'll try again, and if we're hunting for Gregg and aiming to rouse the law in Dalton, he'll try to stop us. We'd better keep our eyes skinned.'

Carlos nodded. 'Maybe Gregg Miller got ambushed?'

I didn't answer for a moment, trying to think of some other explanation for Gregg's disappearance — but there was none. 'It sure looks that way,' I said.

We pushed on and by noon were swinging eastward, the Smokes growing steadily closer. We dismounted by a small stream, watered the horses, and ate the meat which Mattie had packed for us. Afterwards, while we smoked, I realized how close we were to the Shaughnessy homestead. An hour's ride could have me at their cabin.

The idea grew in me. Maybe it was reckless, but the risk seemed worth taking since at that time of day the Shaughnessy menfolk would be out tending their flocks. Wherever Gregg was now, a couple of hours wouldn't make much difference. The prospect of seeing Janet finally decided the issue for me.

I told Carlos what was in my mind. Concern showed in his face. 'I better come with you, Meester Jim.'

I shook my head. 'No sense in us both risking our necks. Wait in those trees upstream. If I ain't back in four hours, ride for Dalton and bring back Shayman.'

He sighed heavily, then said, '*Si, señor.*'

As I rode through the trees, my mind was full of Janet. I was crazy with love, and I wanted to know the truth

I progressed carefully. When I was forced to cross open ground, I kept my rifle unsheathed and ready. Several times I passed scattered flocks of sheep, but they were untended. Sighting three sheepherders' soddies, I took pains to keep well wide of them.

As I'd reckoned, it was one hour after leaving Carlos that I tethered Copper in the trees above the Shaughnessy homestead.

I crouched down and spied out the place. It was a sturdy cabin, with a yard, a barn and a shack. There was also a corral which was empty. Everything was very quiet, the only indication that somebody was at home being the open kitchen door.

After a while Emma Shaughnessy came out, emptied a pail, then returned indoors. I gave her three minutes, then followed her up, silently praying that Brack and Nat were far from home; I pushed my way through the door.

Emma swung round in alarm, but recovering from her shock, she placed the pail on the floor and faced me calmly. Some years back she'd been the prettiest woman around, but the hard life had left its mark on her. Now she reached down a cloth and dried her hands.

'My boys'll kill you if they catch you,' she said.

'Where are they?'

She eyed me. 'Are you alone?' she asked, and when I nodded, she added, 'They're in the hills.'

I relaxed, knowing her to be an honest woman. 'You may not know it, Mrs Shaughnessy,' I said, 'but Janet saved my life. I reckoned it was time I said thanks.'

'I knew,' Emma murmured, 'though Brack and Nathaniel are still wondering who cut you down. I think what they did was a wicked thing — just as all the bloodshed in the valley is wicked. But I must warn you. Every second you delay here you're one step nearer the grave!'

'Where's Janet?' I asked.

She smoothed a wayward curl from her worried eyes. 'Go your way. I'll pass on your thanks.'

'Where is she? I ain't come this way for nothing.'

She hesitated, but then said, 'Janet's

in the barn. Say what you've got to, then for God's sake go . . . '

Nodding my gratitude I went from the cabin to the barn across the yard. Inside, it was cool and fragrant with the scent of straw, and there was a filled pail and a satisfied cow — but otherwise the place was empty.

At the far end was a wide-open door through which I could see the greenery of the slope and trees. I went out that way and glanced about. A ewe and its lamb moved smartly round the side of the barn. A path led into the trees opposite me and I followed it, ducking my head to avoid low-hanging branches. After a minute I detected a movement in the foliage to my left. I brushed my way through, and there was Copper, looking up in puzzlement from his grass-chewing. I cursed and stared around me. The only sound was the chatter of birds above my head.

I was turning to go back the way I'd come, when she called my name and as my gaze was drawn to the soft voice she stepped down from the trees into the clearing.

The sunlight had found a way through the branches to glint in her hair. She was dressed in a thin, cotton work-shirt and slim-fitting blue Levis, and she was bare-footed as she so often had been in the old days.

Like a half-wit, I stood there and gaped, like I always did when it occurred to me how pretty she was.

'Janet, thanks for saving my life,' I gasped.

'It's thanks enough just seeing you alive and well, Jim.' Her voice was little more than a whisper. After an awkward silence, her words came in a breathless rush. 'How is she, Jim? *How is your wife?*'

My mouth dropped open in amazement. Were my ears playing tricks! 'My wife . . . ? I'm not married, Janet. You're the only gal I ever had, or ever wanted!'

'We heard you married some Boston gal . . . '

'That's a damned lie,' I gasped. 'Who said that?'

She shook her head in bewilderment. 'So you're not married?'

'Janet, I wouldn't marry anybody except you. I wrote lots of letters, but never got a single reply.'

She said, 'But I never once heard from you, Jim.'

'I wrote every week — every few days,' I exclaimed. I couldn't understand. It was crazy.

'Oh, Jim, dearest . . . ' She lifted her face, no longer sad. 'Jim . . . Jim . . . ' And her arms were around me, clinging as if she never meant to leave go.

Her lips were quivering and hungry for mine; all the long-denied sweetness of old was suddenly ours.

How long we remained in each other's arms I don't know. When we finally drew apart, the birds' chirruping seemed to echo our happiness. And there was Copper, his forelegs crossed as if he was all set to wait forever.

I kissed Janet again. 'You do believe

you're the only gal for me? That I want to make you my wife?'

'Jim, nothing in the world would make me happier.'

'But what happened to my letters? Somebody must've stolen them.'

Janet shook her head, but my mind got around to Sam Crevis. He'd had reason enough if he fancied Janet himself. Maybe he'd bribed the postmaster. Maybe one day I'd find out the truth.

'You still love me, Janet?' I asked the question just for the pleasure of hearing her say it.

She smoothed my face with the same gentle touch which had guided me through the nightmare journey after the whipping. 'Yes, honey,' she whispered. But when she looked into my eyes the sadness had returned. 'I know you heard rumours about me and Sam Crevis, Jim. But they're all lies. Sam wanted to marry me, and told everybody he was going to. Pa wanted it and tried to talk me into it, but I wouldn't have anything to do with Sam and he turned mean. But surely you'll never marry me now, Jim — not after all the hatred that has come between our families. Not with the thought in your mind that a Shaughnessy might be your father's killer!'

I winced. 'You don't believe that's true?'

'I don't know,' she whispered. 'Jim, I just don't know. Most people seem to think that Brack, Nat and Sam Crevis were near Peakman's Gulley on the day your pa got killed. There's so much hatred and bitterness.'

I hugged her against me. 'What other people think doesn't change the way I feel about you. Maybe your kin hated Pa, but I don't figure they murdered him. I reckon I know who did — and I aim to prove it right soon.'

We both tensed as we heard the pounding of hooves down by the cabin. 'That's Brack,' Janet whispered urgently. 'You must go now. Remember I love you. I always have.'

I gave her a final kiss. 'We'll be married soon.'

Once I was clear of the cabin, I began cutting across the wooded slopes towards the place where I'd left Carlos. My heart was singing with joy. For the first time since my return from the east, I had something tangible to hang on to, something to make the struggle worthwhile.

I was aware of somebody who rose head and shoulders above all our other enemies, somebody with whom must come a deadly reckoning in the very close future — *Wint Craig*.

My immediate aim though was to rejoin Carlos and to push along the Dalton trail. After a quick calculation of the time, I reckoned I'd just make it back to the rendezvous within the four hours. But I hadn't counted on Mitch Edwards and his flock of sheep.

Scattered over the one stretch of open ground I was obliged to cross before reaching the final timberbelt and the stream beyond, they couldn't have been grazing in a worse place for me. Cursing my luck, I eased my horse back into the cover of an ash thicket.

Slumped lazily in his saddle, Edwards was blissfully unaware that a Bannerman was close. I unsheathed my rifle, recalling the fiendish way he'd planned the attack on Hilda Zimm's house, and how he'd stood enjoying the sight of Sam Crevis whipping me.

I had his chunky frame in my sights, but at that moment he turned his horse so his back was towards me. I don't think I'd have shot him anyway, not without giving him the chance to reach for his gun, and least of all in the back. I lowered my rifle.

So I waited until Edwards had driven his sheep on, and that wait cost me a half-hour of precious time.

When I finally reached the upstream trees, Carlos had kept his promise. He was gone up the Dalton trail.

Dusk was settling in as I rode through the pass into the Smoke Mountains. The sombre rock faces rose steeply at my sides, echoing the sound of the chestnut's hooves.

All through the evening, the tracks of a lone horseman had shown in the dust, and now I expected to sight Carlos with each twist of the trail. But with the coming of darkness, I still hadn't caught up with him.

Allowing Copper a rest, I dismounted. I decided to have another check on Carlos's tracks. Surely he couldn't be far ahead now. I struck a match and found what I was looking for. The tracks were clear-cut and recent. About to straighten up, I caught sight of another set of tracks. These were some four yards across the trail, and were pointing towards Dalton. They showed even clearer than Carlos's.

Obviously, up ahead of me, somebody else was trailing the Mexican. Uneasiness came over me, and I quickly rode on. The darkness obscured the tracks, so every few minutes I dismounted and struck a match.

At my third halt, I discovered

the more recent hoof prints had disappeared; Carlos's still remained. I cursed and turned back, leading my horse in the softer ground at the side of the trail so he wouldn't make any noise.

Eventually I found that the second set of tracks had branched off into an arroyo. I remembered that further along, the trail went into a wide loop round the mountainside. This arroyo was the ideal route to put the pursuer ahead of his quarry and into a bushwhacking position.

I left Copper then, and climbed up the arroyo, which twisted steeply through the dense, tangled growth. Pushing my way blindly through the branches, I blundered into a tethered horse — and stood helpless as it shattered the night's silence with its frightened whinny.

I edged to the left and sprawled down, listening. Damn it, I should have realized that my mysterious enemy wouldn't take his animal right up the arroyo. I could hear the horse stomping his feet indignantly and pulling at the fastened reins, but after a while he quietened.

Then, in the silence, a stone clattered and I heard a man curse — alarmingly close. Movement sounded ahead of me. My companion in the darkness was probably puzzled by his horse whinnying, but his lack of caution showed he wasn't aware of my presence — yet. But then his animal repeated its spooked call, and this time, from down on the trail, Copper unleashed an answer!

I crouched down, straining my ears for any sound, and moments later the shadowy, silent hulk of a man appeared a few yards ahead of me, clambering carefully over the rocks. He paused, listening, and then eased himself into the thicket where the horse was tethered. Unholstering my Colt, I went after him . . .

The pale blur of his hat was visible through the trees, and his horse, beginning to wheel again, drowned all sound of my approach until I was within a few yards of him. Then a stone slid away from beneath my boot. The man whipped around, and I caught a glimpse of moon-glinting gun-barrel, but before his finger could tighten on the trigger I had fired, and the pistol went spinning from his grasp. He fell backwards into the bushes, yelping with pain. I sprang after him, but clawing bushes made me miss the mark. Too late I saw him lunging at me, and before I could dodge to the side, he rammed his elbow down onto my skull, knocking me dizzy.

I shook the muzziness from my head and grabbed him. My hands closed over his forearm; he was all slippery with blood and eluded me. Desperate now, I grasped his coat. His knee came up into my groin, but gritting my teeth against the pain, I held on. Then I managed to get a fist free and found space to draw it back. I slammed it into his belly. The breath exploded from his lips. He slumped forward but I switched my grip to his collar and pulled him upright. My next blow took him full on the jaw; this time he went down and stayed down.

For a second I stood there, gasping cool air into my lungs. I felt sticky with my own sweat and his blood. With bruised fingers I fumbled in my pocket and found my matches. I rolled his senseless hulk over, and sparked off a flame. In the light, I found myself looking into the face of Wint Craig's one-eyed confederate.

14

Carlos took a last draw on his cigar and tossed it into our camp-fire. We'd boiled coffee and eaten some more meat. One-Eye lay in the shadows with a rope around his wrists and ankles. He'd lost a lot of blood, my shot having grooved the flesh of his thigh, but we'd bandaged him with the ripped-away leg of his trousers. I didn't feel sorry for him. I was aware of his eye watching me. He'd been sulky and silent so far, but now I was figuring it was time for a bit of talking. I gave Carlos a nod.

The Mexican unsheathed his Kiowa knife; its edge was razor-keen, and now he thrust the blade into the fire and said, 'I've learned many things from the Utes.'

One-Eye glanced up, fear in his face. How different he'd have been had the boot been on the other foot!

Carlos carefully took his knife from the fire; its blade was white-hot. We both stood up.

'Reckon you best start talking, One-Eye,' I said. 'Might help considerable if, when we hand you over to the law in Dalton, we could say, 'This hombre turned honest and told us all he knew.' On the other hand, your face is so ugly that if it got burned, nobody'd be any wiser!'

He swallowed hard, swearing at us. His eye switched from the heated knife-blade to Carlos's hard-set features. He started to tremble. His sort of guts showed up best from behind a rock.

'I'll talk,' he spat out, 'but don't tell Craig!'

I nodded and waited.

He knew a lot. We couldn't be certain he wasn't keeping some back; even so, he gave us plenty to chew on. He claimed he didn't know who'd killed my father. He'd struck up with Craig soon after the gunman had escaped from jail.

Craig, anxious to get a gang together again, had arranged for the rendezvous in Grand Valley, intending at the same time to satisfy his revenge against the Bannermans. But he'd gotten himself tangled with a woman in town — and that woman was Hilda Zimm!

When his bunkies had arrived, they'd been impatient to get the job done — to wreck the Double Horseshoe and ride away — but Frank was paying Craig a tidy sum for his 'protection'. In snivelling tones, One-Eye gave us Craig's reply to his over-eager accomplices . . . *We're staying here awhile. Those sheepherders ain't no paupers now they got the cash for that stolen herd. They got it hidden in their cabins, but we'll find it when the time's ripe. We'll play it Frank Bannerman's way for now. Later, when we're ready, we'll rip this whole goddam valley to bits!*

All One-Eye could tell us of Gregg Miller was that one of Craig's side-kicks, Lew Phillips, had been despatched on the same day as Gregg's departure with orders to make sure no word reached the law in Dalton.

Before Lew Phillips quit the Double Horseshoe, One-Eye heard him mention Broncho Gap as the most likely place for him to set an ambush. By the time Carlos and I had hit out along the Dalton trail, no news of either Lew Phillips or Gregg Miller had reached Craig's ears. One-Eye's orders had been to find out what had happened, after first disposing of Carlos and me.

'You won't tell Craig I talked?' One-Eye pleaded.

'When Craig and I meet it won't be for conversation,' I assured him.

Carlos kicked out the remains of the fire, after which we pulled our captive to his feet and tied him across the back of his horse, then we swung into our own saddles. Soon we were pushing through the darkness.

One hour later we reined-up within the confines of Broncho Gap, Gregg Miller's supposed place of death.

The moon, by now full and very bright, painted the sheer mountainsides a ghostly silver, the light making our search that much easier. Carlos took one side of the gorge, I took the other, and within ten minutes I'd found the body, motionless and sprawled grotesquely, face-down. But it wasn't Gregg Miller's body.

Lew Phillips had been there the best part of a week, a bullet between his eyes. Never a handsome man in life, now thanks to the buzzards he made an ugly corpse.

Cupping my hands to my mouth, I unleashed the wolf-howl that was our means of establishing contact — and soon Carlos came scrambling across the gorge to join me. Staring at the corpse, he said, 'Maybe the deputy came off the best after all, Meester Jim.'

'Then why hasn't he brought the law back from Dalton?' I demanded.

Carlos straightened up from examining the corpse. 'Maybe I know who might help us. From the other side of the pass, I could see into a canyon . . . over that way.' He waved his hand. 'In the canyon were some Ute tepees!'

I nodded. 'Those Utes might have the answers. Ain't no sense in blundering into their camp when it's dark, though. We'll visit them at daybreak.'

Returning to our animals, and our prisoner, we made camp and waited impatiently for the dawn.

★ ★ ★

They were poor as prairie-dogs, vastly different from the proud warriors who had followed Chief Ouray in the old days — yet there was still a dignity about them.

We rode into their encampment as the women were kindling the breakfast fires. They were Yampa Utes, Chief Owl's band. Dogs snapped at our horses, their yap stirring life from within the tepees.

The old chief appeared, standing head high and aloof in our path. He wore a battered Stetson with an eagle feather through its band; his face was wizened. The tribe gathered uneasily behind him, suspicious of us.

We reined in our animals, and Carlos lifted his hand, palm outward, in greeting. 'We come in peace,' he said solemnly, and the chief returned the gesture.

Then Carlos switched to the Ute tongue, which I couldn't understand, recognizing only the mention of Maria's name. This brought an immediate softening in the chief's expression. Maria, a Yampa Ute, had once belonged to Owl's band. The chief spoke and then gestured for us to dismount and follow him. As we did this, Carlos whispered, 'The Indians watched the fight between two white men. The ugly one was killed and they will not go near where he died; they say it's evil. The man with a bright star was wounded badly, and the Indians brought him to their camp.'

We were ushered into a shadowy

tepee. A blanket-covered man rested inside, and his deep breathing told us he was asleep. The old woman crouching over him stood back so we could see his face. It was Gregg Miller.

The Ute woman spoke in English — the hesitant English of one who had perhaps known the company of a white man. 'He . . . walked in the evening for a long time. It was not the Great One's will that he should pass into the land of the spirits.'

'We'll not forget your kindness,' I said. 'There'll always be meat for you when you come to Grand Valley.'

I knelt beside Gregg. His head was bandaged and his wan features indicated that he had lost a lot of blood, but his deep, restful slumber made it clear that he was out of danger. I didn't wake him; I was happy because I knew the old woman was right. Gregg would recover.

We quit the Indian camp, leaving Gregg in their care. In the old Ute woman he had a competent nurse.

As we rode on, I had the harrying feeling that the sands of time were running against us. Wint Craig had promised to 'rip the valley to bits', and he was quite capable of carrying out that threat. He was expecting the remainder of his gang to show up any day now — they might even have arrived since Carlos and I had been away.

I made a decision. Turning to Carlos, I said, 'I'm sure there's nothing to fear from Craig at this end of the trail now. Take One-Eye into Dalton and hand him over to the law. Then get Sheriff Joe Shayman to raise a posse, and lead them hell for leather back to Grand Valley. And, Carlos, pray to God you make it before Craig is wading knee-deep in innocent blood!'

Carlos and I said our farewells, then he and the sorry-looking One-Eye hit out for Dalton. I swung Copper about and heeled him into full gallop. He responded eagerly.

As I raced on, I had a vision of Wint Craig's guns blazing death, and flames licking ravenously through innocent homesteads. Questions pestered me, but now things were beginning to fall into place. Sure enough, I could understand the rift between Frank and Hilda Zimm — but I guessed that my brother had no idea that Craig was the cause of that rift. That day I'd ridden into Coltville to find out what had become of Gregg Miller, I'd fancied somebody had followed me from the Double Horseshoe. It was after I'd passed the Zimm house that signs on my back-trail had disappeared. It all tied in now: the man I'd disturbed in his woman-handling, later that same night, had been Craig. He had a strange hold over many people, including Frank and Marshal Dainton.

A final all-out assault on the sheep-herders would provide Craig with all the ill-gotten cash and loot he wanted from the well-stocked cabins, and with that he'd quit 'playing it Frank Bannerman's way'. When that happened, he'd exact revenge for his years of imprisonment in full.

Although half hoping that Crevis and his men might withstand the final assault, I now knew that once Craig's gang was reinforced, the sheepherders would be no match for them. Unless I could force the truth into Frank's stubborn head, he'd be with Craig all the way, obsessed with the notion that the sheepmen had been responsible for Pa's death. Too late would he realize the truth.

I forced Copper on. I knew that Janet, Mattie, Maria and many more innocent folks were in grave danger.

With the coming of dusk I reached the fringe of the sheepherders' country. I flung caution to the night breeze; no long-trailing via the Coyote Lake range now. My horse's brave but wearying stride carried me unhindered past cabins and flocks of sheep.

It was dark as I forded the river. I

allowed Copper to slake his thirst, and did the same myself. As I straightened up, I fancied I heard hooves, many hooves, pounding behind me in the night. But soon silence returned, so I pushed on again.

When I skirted that final knoll, lights were visible from the Double Horseshoe. I pulled up in the yard, and Frank appeared, holding a lantern, and I could see excitement burning in his eyes. In my haste, I half fell from my saddle and strode towards him.

'Frank,' I gasped, 'I'm sure Wint Craig killed Pa. He's planning to kill us as well.'

'You're wrong,' he said impatiently. 'Them devils across the river did it — I told you afore. Wint's riding with us, and you needn't be feared about his loyalty. I'm paying him mighty well for it!'

For the first time, I noticed Hilda Zimm standing behind Frank in the doorway. Her head was held high and a defiant smile was playing on her lips. I was on the point of blurting out to Frank what I knew about her and Craig, when Mattie called my name.

I stepped across and took hold of her shoulders. 'Gregg's safe,' I told her. 'He was in a gunfight and he's been hurt, but he'll be okay. The Utes are looking after him at their camp along the Dalton trail.'

'Thank God.' Mattie's breath gushed out in relief.

'And Carlos has gone to fetch the law from Dalton.' Before I could say more, I felt a grip like steel around my arm.

I turned to see Frank, his face twisted with anger. 'This war is my business,' he shouted. 'I can handle things by myself. You've done nothing but go against me ever since you got back from the east. I told you if you don't like the way I'm running things, I'll pay top price for your share of the Double Horseshoe . . .'

'You'd like that, wouldn't you, Frank?' I cried. 'Well, you just put it outa your head. I'm staying!'

'I ain't got no time to waste with you,' he countered.

'Listen,' I got out, 'Craig's man, One-Eye, tried to ambush Carlos and me on the way to Dalton. I grabbed him and made him talk. He said Craig was just waiting his chance to destroy the whole valley, us included ...'

'That little one-eyed punk!' Frank laughed. 'I fired him a couple of days ago for being lazy. He swore he'd get even with me. Why don't you grow up, Jim!' He turned and pushed past Hilda, back into the house.

Hearing the sound of horses, I turned to see Ed Hunter, Jess Fulcher and a half-dozen Double Horseshoe men mounting up by the bunk-houses. Frank returned from the house. This time he was carrying a rifle.

'We don't need law from Dalton,' he said. 'When they get here the fighting'll be over and the sheepherders finished.

The rest of Craig's men got here this morning.'

As the significance of those words sank in, I was left speechless. It was already too late.

Frank dropped the level of his voice, trying to reason with me. 'Whatever Craig is, we need him, Jim. There's gonna be hell let loose tonight, and we need him on our side to drive the sheepherders out of this valley. Tonight will see the finish of all our troubles.'

'Where's Craig now?' I asked, fighting back dismay.

'He's taken his boys out to circle round the back of the sheepherders. Me and the rest of our men'll hit them from the front. They won't stand a chance.'

'My God!' I gasped.

Frank shrugged his shoulders and stepped away from me. Jess Fulcher had his horse saddled and ready, and he mounted up. 'If you want a part in this fight,' he called over his shoulder, 'you can ride after us!' With that he waved his men forward and they left the ranch.

I watched them go, then led Copper into the stable and unsaddled him. Minutes later I was mounted up on the dun-pony and spurring him out into the yard.

Mattie came running towards me, but I waved her aside. 'I'm going with Frank,' I shouted. 'Maybe there's something I can do, though God knows what!'

It took me fifteen minutes to catch them up. As I pulled alongside Frank, he turned and grinned.

'I'm glad you're riding with us, Jim,' he cried above the thud of hooves. 'The whole valley'll be ours after tonight — and Pa'll be revenged!'

I nodded, only half listening. Inwardly I was pleading that I'd find some means of saving Janet.

We thundered across the prairie, while somewhere ahead of us Wint Craig was making his curving advance to get behind the sheepherders. But Frank hadn't taken into consideration that this very same night was one for which Sam Crevis had planned an attack.

15

As we approached the point where I'd crossed the river earlier that night, we could hear the roar of gunfire from upstream. We reined in and listened to the wild, deadly cadence and Frank cursed because the shooting wasn't part of his plan, leastways not at this stage.

'Sounds as if Wint's run into trouble,' he said. ' 'Bout a mile upstream, I guess.'

'Must be around Pine Creek,' grunted Jess Fulcher. Frank nodded, frowning thoughtfully.

Would it be best to quit Frank, I wondered, and ride to the Shaughnessys with a warning? Then I realized that knowing where Craig was now, I might be able to get at him before he broke through the sheepherders at Pine Creek; disaster might yet be avoided. So, when Frank made up his mind to cross the river and follow along the far bank to the scene of conflict, I went with him.

The fury of the firing increased as we neared the creek. We rode on to the stony flat which flanked the river. The bank on our right curled up sharply to form a lip, beyond which the land sloped towards the pines.

We dismounted, keeping behind the cut of the bank, and from up ahead, alongside the river, I could hear men's curses intermingled with the crack of gunfire. Frank raised his arm, and we pulled in. 'That's Craig up there for sure,' he whispered hoarsely.

'And the sheepherders are up in those pines,' Ed Hunter said.

Frank reached forward to unsheath his rifle. 'Wait here,' he commanded. 'I'm gonna crawl up there to Wint and see what he reckons is the best thing to do.' He moved out, not waiting for any response.

We crouched on the stones and waited. The gunplay continued unabated, but it was soon plain that most of the fire was coming from the men lining the river. Within ten minutes Frank returned; his meeting with Craig had re-kindled his enthusiasm.

'Wint says we're to crawl up to where he is now and then open fire,' he informed us. 'He's taking his boys north; he'll swing round behind the pines and catch them from the back, as we planned. He'll call out when it's safe for us to climb the slope, and we'll regroup in the pines.'

Jess Fulcher grabbed the horses. There were seven men, not counting Jess, Frank and me, and these began to move towards the point where Frank had indicated they should open fire from. I dodged past the dun-pony and clawed at Frank's arm, pulling him round to face me.

'Send those men up across that open ground,' I cried, 'and you'll be sending them to their deaths. Craig's guns'll pick 'em off easy as anything.'

'Craig's on our side, damn you!' Frank snarled. 'Come on, man!' And he was gone after the others.

But instead of following him, I backed past the amazed Jess Fulcher, who was holding the horses, and scrambled along the river-bank. If somehow I could get to Craig, if I could put a bullet between his eyes . . .

Having made my way downstream for a hundred yards, I pulled in and listened. It was impossible to tell whether Frank had taken over the firing from Craig's men; there had been no slackening of noise. I climbed the bank and started up the slope. Halfway up, and with the battle raging well to my left, any doubts I'd had about the whereabouts of Wint Craig were settled as the sudden clamour of fresh gunfire broke out from behind the pines. Wint Craig and his killers had made it round the back!

A voice that might have been Nat Shaughnessy's yelled out, 'They're behind us, by God!' Three men broke from the trees, only to fall in the cross-whip of lead to which Frank's men now contributed with murderous effect.

I climbed for another twenty yards, unnoticed I hoped, in the darkness, then I turned towards the pines.

From the trees came the sound of men grappling with each other, accompanied by the snap of hand-guns. Again, sheepherders burst clear of the pines, only to be shattered by a fusillade from the men along the river-bank.

Moving closer, I glimpsed spurts of flame amid the trees, and momentarily, the silhouettes of running men.

Presently, the gunfire slackened and then died out completely. Soon the only sound was the murmur of the night breeze. Suddenly the moon decided to escape the cloud, and its light bathed the slope, revealing the dark hulks of men's bodies sprawled upon the ground.

Anger hit me. This had been wholesale butchery; the victims had stood no chance. The sheepherders had been crushed in absolute defeat.

As I neared the forest, Craig's voice sounded: 'Okay, Frank, come on up. Let's get to their cabins!'

The sound of hooves down by the river warned me that Frank was having his horses brought up, and soon I could see the dark shapes of mounted men urging their animals over the lip of the bank.

In desperation I yelled with all my strength: 'For God's sake get back! *Craig'll kill you*!'

The Double Horseshoe hands hesitated, some turning back, others stopping in their tracks, but I was unable to tell if Frank was among them. Suddenly the gunfire was crashing out from the trees, with Wint Craig's screamed 'Get 'em, boys!' lifting into the bedlam. Backing the gunfire came the pounding of hooves as Craig's henchmen charged down towards Frank's men.

I ploughed into the pines, frantically conscious of the renewed massacre down-slope. Then the firing died out, and with horror I suspected that Frank and his followers had suffered the same fate as the sheepherders.

Tripping over something soft in the darkness, I reached down to feel a man's body. Fresh blood was on my hand as I withdrew it. He was lying face down in a small clearing. The moon was slanting beams of silver through the branches. I rolled the body over, dragging the face round so it was out of the shadow. Here was Mitch Edwards, looking ghastly in his death. As I straightened up, the hammer-click of a six-shooter sounded!

Fifteen feet from me, black and formidable in the moonlight, with gun directed at me, stood Wint Craig. He chuckled quietly. 'Jim Bannerman. Get your hands up!'

My arms felt like lead weights as I lifted them.

He said, 'I've sweated a long time to get at you. Now I don't even have to make it look like an accident!'

'An accident?' My voice seemed far

off, as if it didn't belong to me. 'Like being crushed by a boulder?'

The laugh came again. 'You kinda set yourself up for that. Had I known it was you that night at Hilda's, I guess I'd have lingered awhile. Mighty considerate of you to bring her back to the Double Horseshoe, though.'

He edged forward, impatient to finish me; but I had another question. 'You killed Pa, didn't you, Craig?'

He leaned forward slightly; I could sense his finger tightening on the trigger. 'I'll grant you that much satisfaction before you die . . . Yes, I killed him!'

So now I knew, and sickened I braced myself for the bullet — suddenly Brack Shaughnessy reared out of the shadows, the gun in his hand stabbing flame — at Craig!

The killer yelled in anguish as lead ripped into him, but he swung his own weapon, its roar sounding twice, driving Brack down before he could fire again.

Everything had happened so rapidly. Instinctively, I hurled myself back into the trees. My own Colt was in my hand and I blasted off three shots in Craig's direction. Lead splintered the tree-trunk inches from my head, and more shots ripped through the branches above. I emptied my gun into the shadows on the edge of the clearing, and then I heard shouting and the movement of horses approaching through the foliage. The rest of Craig's gang were returning from the butchery down-slope.

I started to run, twisting through the trees, my feet making no sound on the pine-needles. The voices grew fainter behind me and there were no more shots, and suddenly I was out of the forest. Down-slope, the river glinted beneath the moon and I lunged towards it. Maybe there were still some horses down there. Mounted, it wouldn't take me long to reach the Shaughnessy cabin.

I paused, listening for sound of

pursuit — but there was nothing. Maybe my enemies figured I hadn't survived the shooting. Maybe Wint Craig was dead and they were too preoccupied. Cheered by that prospect, I ran on.

I hit the cut-away of the bank earlier than expected. I was over it and plunging down before I realized this was its steepest point. My clawing hands ripped bushes out by the roots, but I crashed down, showering myself with earth, and rolled over and over. Then my head cracked against a rock. I was faintly aware that I was no longer falling, but by then I was waging a frantic battle to pull clear of clogging mists. I felt my senses slipping away and knew I had lost that battle.

★ ★ ★

I became aware of the cool breeze; then I heard the ripple of the river. I realized that the sky had lost its stars. I groaned. My head felt awful.

My wound had split open again, and my shirt was soggy with blood.

I gazed to the east where the land-ridge was tinted with the pinkness of dawn. As all the memories of the night flooded back to me, I staggered on to my feet.

I began to walk along the river-bank. I came across a dead horse. Nearby I discovered Jess Fulcher. He was sprawled across a boulder. His eyes were open, but they'd ceased to see anything. His shirt-front was torn to bloody shreds where shots had ploughed into him.

I could have gone further along the river-bank, but I figured I'd seen enough of death. There was nothing living here, neither man nor beast. But what of the sheepherders' families? What of Janet?

Climbing away from the water, I looked towards the pines, but they were shadowy and silent. I trudged up the hill, skirting the forest and dipping into the valley beyond. I was too weary to seek cover, too weary to care very much if somebody was planning to take a shot at me.

Eventually, I came across some sheep, and these ran off, splitting the silence with their stupid bleating.

The breeze had dropped and the new day was growing stronger as I reached the first cabin — what was left of it. The mass of angled beams, blackened and still smouldering, had once been the home of the Edwards' family. A shroud of smoke still hung low over the place.

I heard a woman sobbing, and turning saw Nell Edwards standing on the churned-up earth which had once been a flower-garden. Two children were clinging to her skirts and she was holding a shotgun which was pointed at me. I walked towards her, remembering the corpse of her husband which I'd stumbled over in the pines.

'Put your gun away, woman,' I murmured. 'There's been enough shooting, enough killing.'

Slowly the gun lowered, and then she sank to the ground, her body shuddering with long, rasping sobs. After a moment she stopped and raised her tearful face. 'Mitch . . . ?' she whispered. 'Is he . . . ?'

Strangely, when I'd told her, she seemed to pull herself together, as though self-control came easier now that her last hopes were shattered. She dried her eyes.

'All this sadness is no good for the kids,' she said.

I noticed that the ground was littered with pulled-out drawers, bits of furniture and clothing which had been ransacked out of the cabin before it was burned.

'How long ago did it happen?' I asked.

'Four — five hours.' Her voice was low and flat. 'About fifteen of them, there were. Their leader was a man called Craig. He was wounded and bleeding hard — but that didn't stop them from doing this.'

I did what I could for Nell Edwards, which was little enough. I gave her my coat, then told her to start out for Coltville. I had a little money on me and I pushed it into her hand. In town she'd have enough to pay for a room while she made up her mind what to do. She thanked me with resignation more than gratitude, then took her children and trudged away.

An hour later I was nearing the Shaughnessy homestead. I knew what I'd find even before I'd topped that last rise: *A gutted ruin, still smouldering red, within which it would be impossible to distinguish human ash from wood ash!*

The blackened stone chimney-stack reared like a giant tomb-stone above the mess. The cow lay bullet-riddled amid the discarded belongings which had been ripped out of the cabin by Craig and his murderers. They had taken anything of value — but I found a cotton dress down there; it had frills and even amid all this ugliness it seemed strangely pretty. It had been Janet's.

I lay down upon the earth, bitterness and sorrow sweeping over me. Eventually exhaustion caught up with me and I slept.

16

I awoke. The sun was directly overhead. I glanced across at the gutted homestead. I felt sick. It seemed I'd failed Janet and accomplished nothing.

I climbed to my feet. Nowhere could I see a sign of movement. There was nothing I could do here now. I thought about Mattie, Maria and the kids back at the Double Horseshoe, and wondered if Craig had spread devastation on that side of the river as well. Fearful of what awaited me, I started out on the long walk home.

It was mid-afternoon when I quit the timber and made my way towards the river. I was caked with sweat and the prospect of cool water had me quickening my pace.

Then suddenly I heard the thud of hooves from beyond a rise to my left. I glanced around for a hiding-place, but the ground was open and the grass sheep-nibbled.

When the riders topped the ridge, I was standing gun in hand, ready to make a last-ditch stand. I slipped the gun back into its holster. Carlos gave a surprised shout of greeting. Backing him was a short, stubby man wearing a law badge, while behind him rode a posse of horsemen.

Carlos reined his animal alongside me and dismounted, but his smile changed to a frown as I told him what had happened. He gestured towards the stubby lawman. 'This here is Sheriff Joe Shayman from Dalton.'

Shayman leaned forward and shook my hand. His grip was firm. His jacket was sagging open, leaving the forward-jutting butt of his Colt within unhampered reach. His eyes were narrowed and determined.

'Too bad we didn't get here a day earlier, Mister Bannerman,' Shayman grunted. 'But we'll get Wint Craig, I give you my word, even if we have to trail him clear across the territory. If he's wounded, it may not be such a long trail. Now let's make tracks for the Double Horseshoe. Ain't much we can do this side of the river.'

Carlos climbed into his saddle and I mounted up behind, then we hit out for the ranch. Shayman had brought a dozen men with him, all heavily-armed; he clearly didn't intend going back to Dalton empty-handed.

As we drew nearer the ranch, my fear increased. We passed groups of slaughtered cattle, the ground dark with blood. Shayman urged us to greater speed, and all the time I was wondering if we would find the Double Horseshoe a smouldering ruin.

We had almost reached the final knoll when a lone horseman showed up ahead, setting his mount at a fast gallop in our direction. I recognized Copper before I realized who was riding him, but as they drew nearer I could see Frank was in the saddle. As he reached us, he reined to a halt, and his face was white and haggard. 'Thought you were dead, Jim,' he gasped.

'Well, I'm not,' I said, 'but I figured you were!'

'When Craig opened fire on us,' he explained, 'me and Ed Hunter got our horses shot from under us. We got hold of your dun-pony, Jim, and swam him across the river. The two of us mounted up on him and got clear. I think we was the only survivors.'

Shayman got us moving again, and then swung in close so that he could hear my brother's words.

'We got back to Double Horseshoe,' Frank went on. 'I kept watch. I was scared Craig would come to the ranch. He showed up around seven this morning. We heard him shooting up cattle first, and Ed got Mattie, Maria and the kids up into the trees on the knoll. I joined them, after getting the horses outa the stables.

'From the knoll we saw everything. Craig stayed on his horse in the yard while the others ransacked the house. They were in there for maybe ten minutes, ripping the place apart, and all the time, Craig sat there, slumped forward in the saddle and looking mighty sick.

'When the rest had got what they wanted from the house, they lit torches and threw them on to the roof and into the stables. Then they pulled out, moving towards Coltville. We got down off the knoll and put the fires out in the house, but the stables were burned to hell.'

'Mattie and Maria are okay then?' I gasped.

'Sure,' he nodded. 'But I dunno where Hilda's gone. Mattie said she rode out during the night.'

'Have you seen the Shaughnessys — Janet?' I asked.

'Nothing,' he grunted.

I'd been nursing the hope that somehow Janet had escaped the flames of the homestead, but now even that seemed crushed. Yet I refused to accept she was dead. I wouldn't rest until I knew the truth. And Wint Craig and his gang were the only ones who could give me the answer.

The ranch was in a real mess, just as Frank had said. The roof was scorched, the stables gutted and the house ransacked. But all that was of minor importance; what most mattered was that the women and kids were safe. Mattie was soon in evidence, brave as ever. Before long she and Maria had rustled up food and coffee for us all.

Carlos stayed with the women to lend a hand bringing some sort of order to the house. I was astride Copper again as we struck out along the Coltville trail. Shayman set a hot pace. Frank found himself another mount and he rode alongside me. Several times he tried to speak, but he seemed confused. He looked haggard and worried. At last he got his words out.

'Suppose it ain't much good me saying I'm sorry, Jim, and that you was right all along?'

'It's a bit late now,' I said. 'Wint Craig killed our pa, but it was your doing that got all those men killed at Pine Creek.'

'But I figured . . . ' He slumped down in his saddle.

I couldn't raise much sympathy for him; it was too late to be sorry and too late to have second thoughts. After a time, he drew himself up. 'We'll get Craig,' he said as if to ease his conscience.

It was turned six in the evening when we neared Coltville. Craig had obviously skirted the town, pushing into the open country beyond, and Shayman did likewise. But I split with the posse and kept to the trail. If, by a miracle, Janet was still alive, she might have come into Coltville. However, I was disappointed; nobody in the stores or hotel had seen the Shaughnessys. I went to the marshal's office, but it was deserted.

I caught up with the posse as darkness was falling; Craig's trail

238

was showing up fresh and beckoning, and Shayman told me he'd found bloodstains near a stream where the gang had rested. We pushed on into the night, stopping only for an occasional breather.

It was in the small hours when we left the foothills of the Hawk Mountains, and in the broad valley stretching before us were several pin-points of light.

As we milled to a stop around Shayman, he pointed. 'That's the village of Mesilla down yonder. There's a doctor there, and Craig's bad hit. I've been figuring.' He cupped his saddle-pommel, his brow furrowed in concentration. We waited for his decision. After a minute, he straightened up and pointed down at the snaky line of the road into the village which showed silver in the moonlight. Then he turned to one of his men.

'Grant, take six boys and mosey up the road. Keep to the sides and outa sight as much as possible. Hole up about a hundred yards this side of the village and prepare yourselves for a fight.' He raised himself in his stirrups, speaking louder. 'The rest come with me.'

Grant and his six had dismounted and were melting into the shadows lining the road as the remainder of us spurred forward. Shayman edged in close and grunted, 'I'm gonna look a doggone fool if this don't pay off.'

He swung us to the north and we moved cross-prairie, away from Mesilla; eventually we curved round to circle it at a mile radius. The scattered lights were behind us when next he ordered us to halt. 'We'll leave the horses here,' he said. 'We're going in on foot!'

One of our men stayed with the animals, while the rest of us found the road that led back into the village and followed along it. Soon we were passing a few outlying adobe buildings, all of which were in darkness. The sound of our footsteps was muffled by the thick dust.

With Shayman a few yards ahead of

Frank and me and the rest following, we reached the main street. A few lamps showed through the curtained windows of the adobes.

Shayman raised his arm and we pulled in around him. From up the street came the restless stomp of a horse.

The lawman's grit-hard voice came as a whisper. 'You two Bannermans, Hawkins and Reno come with me. The rest of you, wait here five minutes, then spread out and comb through the village and out along the road towards Grant. You'll drive any of Craig's men that are here into his guns if things work out as I hope.'

'Where's the doc's place?' I cut in.

'Up the street, where the horse is rail-hitched. And there's a light showing in the window.'

We checked our guns, keeping them unholstered, and Shayman turned with final instructions to the men we were leaving behind. 'If you hear shooting, come hell for leather!' Then to us, he said, 'Okay, let's go.'

He led us off the street and we passed between the darkened adobes which lined it. From within the walls of these houses came the deep-breathing of sleeping folk.

Somehow I sensed now that Craig was close at hand. The old churning in my belly left me in no doubt. I glanced sideways at Frank. His face showed white.

We came round the back of the doctor's adobe and pulled in, hardly daring to breathe. Again there came the nervous stomp of the horse — and then the sound of a half-stifled cough. A man was standing on the verandah.

Shayman jerked himself forward and we rushed around the building. A thick-set figure, his right arm in a sling, was twisting around, his left hand reaching for the pistol at his side. His draw was swift, but we had the advantage of surprise and Shayman fired. The man was hammered back onto the planking, sprawling in the lantern-glow. It was

Marshal Jim Dainton!

From behind, the rest of our men came charging up, but by now Shayman had wrenched open the door of the house and was barging through, gun first. We followed.

Inside, a solitary old man turned his fear-filled eyes upon us. 'There was n-nothing I could do,' he stuttered. 'He'd . . . he'd lost too much blood!' And then he gasped as his gaze was drawn to Shayman's law badge. 'You're not Craig's men!' he gasped.

'No Doc Freeburg, we ain't,' Shayman grunted, and we brushed past the doctor towards an inner room from which a woman's grief-stricken sobs sounded.

The sheriff kicked the door open, and there, beneath the light of an oil-lamp, on his back across a table, was Wint Craig. His shirt had been ripped away to expose the raw, bloody mess of his chest and side. He was dead.

Hilda Zimm was leaning over him, her yellow hair draped in his blood, and great sobs were shuddering through her body.

In the background, Doc Freeburg was stammering, 'He was n-near gone when they brought him here. I . . . I got the shells outa him, but he'd been bleeding for hours. God knows how he kept going as long as he did. They said, if I let him die, they blast Mesilla to bits . . . but no doctor could've saved him . . .'

He tailed off as gunfire sounded from the outskirts of the village.

Hilda Zimm lifted her anguished face and her lips were drawn back from her teeth like a snarling animal. Her eyes locked with Frank's.

'All your fault!' she hissed. 'All this murdering and thieving. *I hate you, Frank Bannerman!*'

Frank's eyes were burning. He sprang at her, grabbing her blouse, wrenching her to her feet. The back of his hand smashed across her face, then he hurled her against the wall. 'You two-timing bitch!' He'd have gone after her, probably killed her, had I not somehow got my arms around him and dragged him back. Shayman was screaming at Frank to leave her alone, but then Hilda was pushing herself up, her fingers touching the ugly red weals forming across her chalk-white face. She was glaring at Frank, but her screeched words were meant for us all. They stunned the whole room into silence.

'That's the last time you'll ever hit me, Frank Bannerman! Wint told me a lot about you afore he died — about how you wanted Grand Valley for yourself, not caring a damn for anybody else. Wint told me how well you paid him to kill your own pa too. You hadn't the guts to do it yourself!'

I didn't hear the rest of what she was saying because I'd heard enough, and my brain was suddenly spinning with the shock of terrible realization.

Frank jerked from my grasp, backing against the wall, his gun turned upon us. He was panting and snarling, his eyes seething with hatred.

'*You had Pa murdered*!' My screamed accusation was still disbelieving.

He nodded, his lips twisting into a sardonic grin. 'You damned fool, Jim,' he snarled. 'I gave you plenty of chance to clear out, but you hounded me. Yeah, I got Pa killed, so I guess killing you won't come so hard . . . '

Footsteps sounded from beyond the outer door. Frank hesitated, his eyes wavering. Shayman's hand streaked for his gun, its thunderous roar filling the room.

Frank never made a sound. He twisted slightly, the Colt slipping from his fingers, then he plunged down.

I staggered to him, dropped to my knees. A circle of blood was staining his shirt. In death, his expression looked like a maniac's. I shuddered. My father's assassin had been hired by my own brother. I told myself that it wasn't true, that it was a crazy nightmare.

But it was true, and all the convincing in the world would never change that. I buried my face in my hands, blinded by grief — grief not for Frank, but for Pa, and his pride in a son who wasn't worth a damn!

Shayman's man Grant came into the room, but in my anguish I heard only snatches of what he said. 'They rode right into our guns . . . We shot three of them before the rest gave themselves up . . . '

His voice was far off. What he was saying seemed unimportant . . .

17

One of the prisoners — one of Craig's gang — answered my questions. His voice was grudging, but his words were sweet music to me. 'There wasn't nobody in the Shaughnessy cabin when we hit it,' he said.

Janet was alive. The hope grew inside me, till I'd convinced myself that it was a sure-fire certainty.

I'd quit Joe Shayman and his posse at Coltville. I told him to give my share of the reward for Wint Craig's death to help the widowed folk of this tragic war.

Again I'd asked questions in Coltville; still I got no satisfaction. No Shaughnessys had been seen in town.

Now, in the evening, Copper plodded up the trail towards the Double Horseshoe. The land was quiet, seeming to have forgotten the violence. I knew

I'd never forget it.

During the journey back from Mesilla, I tried to fit the pieces of the story together, but I guessed certain things would remain a mystery — buried with the dead.

Just what, I wondered, had drawn Hilda Zimm to Wint Craig? I'd once figured Hilda hadn't a grain of real compassion in her, but the outlaw's death had her weeping and grieving like maybe nothing else ever had.

I suddenly noticed that a man was sitting his horse directly across my trail some thirty yards ahead. As I drew nearer, he made no attempt to clear the way. My hand closed over the butt of my Colt; it was Sam Crevis!

He raised his arm in greeting as I rode up. There was no sign of enmity in his face, just overwhelming tiredness. I watched him warily.

'I've been waiting for you to show up, Jim,' he said quietly. 'I wanted to tell you that Grand Valley is all yours now. There'll be no more sheepherding here.'

'I thought you'd been killed at Pine Creek,' I said.

'Most of us was,' he murmured. 'My brother, Mitch Edwards, Paddy Mulheron, Nat and Brack Shaughnessy. A few got out by playing possum — making out we was dead.'

I still didn't trust him. Memories of the awful things he'd done were too vivid in my mind.

But his tone was strangely humble. 'I wanted to say how mighty sorry I am for the whipping we gave you. If I'd taken you to see old man Shaughnessy, things might've been a whole lot different. He'd have had sense enough to see reason. All I know now is that after the few of us that survived had spaded our kin into the earth, we decided there could be no more sheepherding in this valley — not after all that'd happened. We've got to find someplace new.'

'Where's Janet Shaughnessy?' I asked.
He hesitated. 'I got something for

you, Jim.' I watched him like a hawk, resting my hand on my gun, as he undid his saddle-bag and pulled out two bundles of string-tied envelopes. 'I bribed Seth Williams the postmaster to hold on to all the mail between you and Janet. It's all here. I never had a chance with Janet anyway. You were the only one she loved.'

I took the bundles. I felt anger rising inside me; then I looked at his face and thought he wasn't worth getting het up about.

He leaned forward in his saddle and extended his work-soiled hand. 'Reckon we should've done this years ago, Jim — but at least let's shake now.'

I looked down at the hand that had lashed me near to death; the hand that would have murdered me a hundred times over if the chance had arisen; the hand that had broken my heart with an evil bribe. Then I recalled how I had urged my horse over his body, how I had shot him from his mount on another occasion, and the many times I'd wished him dead.

Maybe I was a fool — but I reached out and shook.

He drew back from my path. He said, 'She's waiting for you at the Double Horseshoe!'

Copper was suddenly leaping forward with a new energy.

Janet was running out to meet me long before I reached the house, her cry of happiness carrying clearly in the still of evening. Way behind her, in the yard of the ranch, was a wagon; in it were seated her parents. In a few hours they'd lost two sons, their home, their livelihood. I promised myself I'd find them a place to live in this valley. Also, I was going to build a secure future for Carlos and his family. As for Mattie, I knew she'd be far away up the Dalton trail by this time, searching for a certain Ute village.

When Janet was about five yards from me, she stopped. Her eyes were red and tearful, her face full of sadness, but her gaze met mine and a valiant smile touched her lips. I dismounted, and she reached out and gripped my arm. 'I'll never let you go again, Jim,' she vowed. 'Never!'

'Janet,' I said, having difficulty in controlling my emotion, 'we'll build us a new Grand Valley. We'll make it a good place to live in.'

She came to me, firm and loving and for always. 'Yes, Jim . . . Oh, *we* will!'

THE END

We do hope that you have enjoyed reading this large print book.

Did you know that all of our titles are available for purchase?

We publish a wide range of high quality large print books including: **Romances, Mysteries, Classics, General Fiction, Non Fiction and Westerns.**

Special interest titles available in large print are: **The Little Oxford Dictionary Music Book, Song Book Hymn Book, Service Book**

Also available from us courtesy of Oxford University Press: **Young Readers' Dictionary (large print edition) Young Readers' Thesaurus (large print edition)**

For further information or a free brochure, please contact us at: **Ulverscroft Large Print Books Ltd., The Green, Bradgate Road, Anstey, Leicester, LE7 7FU, England. Tel:** (00 44) **0116 236 4325 Fax:** (00 44) **0116 234 0205**

TRAIL OF THE CIRCLE STAR

Lee Martin

Finding his cousin, friend, and mentor, Marshal Bob Harrington, hanging dead from a cottonwood tree is a cruel blow for Deputy U.S. Marshal Hank Darringer. He'd like nothing better than to exact a bitter and swift revenge, but as a lawman he knows he must haul the murderers to justice — legally. But seeking justice is tougher than obstructing it in Prospect, Colorado. Hank has to keep one hand on his gun and one eye on his back.

MCKINNEY'S REVENGE

Mike Stotter

When ranch-hand Thadius McKinney finds his newly-wedded wife in the arms of his boss, the powerful, land-hungry Aaron Wyatt, something inside him snaps. Two gunblasts later, McKinney is forced to flee into the night with the beef-baron's thugs hot on his trail, baying for his blood. A man cannot run forever, and even when his back-trail is littered with bodies, the fighting isn't over. McKinney decides it is time for Wyatt to pay the Devil.

THE BROTHERS DEATH

Bill Wade

Russ Hartmann was a wandering cowboy who had seen better days. Two riders followed him out of the past: one brought good news, the other brought murder and disaster. When the Brothers Death took a hand, it appeared certain that Hartmann would go under. But a ranching lady coveted his skill with a gun, and he went to work for her. Slowly he dug both Evelyn Cross's Broken C and himself out of trouble — but he kept the undertaker busy in the process.

RHONE

James Gordon White

Former bounty hunter Phil Rhone finds himself in a mess of trouble when he agrees to help Brad Miller to find his abducted wife, Lorna. They team up with Susan Prescott, a blonde beauty seeking the killers of her family. The hunt takes them up into the isolated mountains to a slave labour gold mine, where they confront sadistic Nelson Forbes. The odds are against them, but Susan thirsts for revenge and Miller isn't leaving without his wife . . .